Blissymbolics

Elizabeth S. Helfman

BLISSYMBOLICS

Speaking Without Speech

ELSEVIER / NELSON BOOKS   New York

DYNIX 146257

212768

Text copyright © 1981 by Elizabeth S. Helfman
Blissymbolics used herein copyright © Blissymbolics Communication Institute 1981 Toronto, Canada

Ⓑ indicates 1) a symbol which differs from the C.K. Bliss version either in symbol form or accompanying wording or 2) a new B.C.I. symbol authorized in the absence of requested comment from C.K. Bliss

Library of Congress Cataloging in Publication Data

Helfman, Elizabeth S
  Blissymbolics, speaking without speech.

  Bibliography: p.
  Includes index.
  1. Pasigraphy. 2. Handicapped—Means of communication. 3. Bliss, Charles Kasiel.
I. Title.
Z102.H44   001.56   80–20431
ISBN 0–525–66678–8

Published in the United States by Elsevier-Dutton Publishing Co., Inc., 2 Park Avenue, New York, N.Y. 10016. Published simultaneously in Don Mills, Ontario, by Nelson/Canada.
Printed in the U.S.A.   First Edition
10 9 8 7 6 5 4 3 2 1

For all the Blissymbol children

Acknowledgments

It would be impossible to mention by name all the people who have helped with the preparation of this book. I am grateful especially to the symbol users, both children and adults, who have found a way into the world by "talking" with Blissymbols. Their courage and their hope inspired me.

Special thanks are also due to Shirley McNaughton and her associates at the Blissymbolics Communication Institute, without whose help the book could not have been written.

Symbols as printed in this book were prepared by the Blissymbolics Communication Institute, holders of the copyright, and have been reproduced with their permission. The address of the Institute, as well as a listing of international resource centers, can be found in the Appendix.

Explanation of letter corrections
In order to reflect individual creativity and different styles of expression, material from symbol users has been reproduced essentially as it was received. However, where appropriate, symbols from display boards of 1975 or earlier have been updated to the current stamp form, produced by the B.C.I. in 1978.

These conversations and letters are not to be regarded as models for expression or instruction.

NOTE: Throughout this book I have used the pronouns *he* or *his* in referring to people of both sexes. To have said *he or she* and *his or her* each time would have been awkward.

Contents

Blast-Off!

A Symbol Poem

I'm pretending I'm going on the moon.

10 9 8 7 6 5 4 3 2 1

Blast-off!

(fire)

I'm going here and there and here and

there and here and there.

10 **9** 8 7 6 5 4 3 2 1

Blast-off!

I'm pretending I'm going home here and there

I'm pretending I'm going in the cloud.

10 9 8 7 6 5 4 3 2 1

Blast-off!

I'm pretending I'm going in the weather.

10 9 8 7 6 5 4 3 2 1

Blast-off!

No more story.

Poem by Kari Harrington

·1·

Language Makes Us People

Seven-year-old Kari Harrington watched as her five-year-old sister, Linda, tried to get the last bit of catsup out of a narrow-necked bottle. Linda shook it and shook it, but nothing came out. The other members of the family were busy eating dinner, and no one seemed to notice. Linda started to cry. Then Kari had an idea and began to wave her left arm. When Linda's attention was caught, Kari pointed at some designs on a board beside her plate.

Linda stopped crying. "What's Kari saying?"

Mrs. Harrington looked to see what Kari was pointing at. "She says, 'Put water in it.'"

The other Harringtons looked at one another in astonishment. Kari's brother was the first to recover from surprise. "Hey, good idea, Kari!" he exclaimed.

"Bravo, Kari!" her father added, as Linda ran to the kitchen to get some water.

Her mother could not manage speech. Instead, she gave Kari a big hug.

Something incredible had just happened—much more than a bright little girl making a practical suggestion. Kari had never before, in all her seven years, made any intelligible comment of any kind. She could not talk.

Kari had been born with a serious form of cerebral palsy, and she could not walk or speak or move any part of her body very well. She spent most of her waking hours in a wheelchair. Some things Kari *could* do—she could see, she could hear, she could move her left arm and hand enough to point, though she could not make signs with her fingers the way deaf people do.

A few months before, Kari had begun learning the meaning of some printed symbols she could use for communication instead of spoken words. So when Linda asked, "What's Kari saying?" she meant, "What symbols is Kari pointing at?"

Learning these symbols meant, for Kari, the end of years of silence broken only by the incomprehensible sounds she made in desperate attempts to speak. It was the end of years of bottling up her feelings of loneliness and frustration. Now she could say "I love you" or "I'm angry."

Kari was not the only one to be taught the symbols. Other children who could not speak were also learning them, in the same special school where Kari went in her wheelchair every day. The discovery of these symbols was the beginning of a bright new world for people whose loneliness and isolation had seemed endless as they struggled to reach out to others but just could not make themselves understood.

This book tells about how these symbols came into existence and how they have helped nonspeaking people, both children and adults, to enter the world of human relationships. But first we will explore, briefly, the story of language and the ways in which it makes us truly human. We will take a look at international languages that have attempted to break down the barrier between people of different tongues. And we will see how all this led to Blissymbolics and how these symbols have meant an end to isolation for people who could not speak.

Our world is changing fast. News flashes across the airways. Satellites in space bring us television pictures of events thousands of miles away. As never before, people in one part of the world know about what is happening in other places. Thousands wing their way through the air in swift airplanes, crossing vast oceans in just a few hours.

Only a hundred years ago, none of this was possible. Relatively few people then traveled far from home. The pioneers who crossed North America to settle in the Far West seldom returned to the East. (To "go west" was a euphemism for dying.) People were concerned mainly with what went on in their own villages. Next in importance was their county or state, then their country, especially in time of trouble. People who had emigrated from Europe were concerned also about the mother country. But the other side of the world was a far, mysterious place about which little was known. At the beginning of the twentieth century, only one person in fifty was likely to travel anywhere beyond the boundaries of his own country. Today, roughly one out of ten will make such a journey. By the end of this century, the ratio of such travelers may be one out of two.

Americans today, like people everywhere, want to know what is happening in the far north and the far south of the world. They want news not only of Europe, but of Asia, Africa, South America, even of Antarctica. There is widespread interest in the everyday lives of people thousands of miles away. How do they cope with problems? What games do they play? How do they express themselves in art, in dance, in music? What are their beliefs about God and the universe?

Countries trade with faraway countries. The price of oil in Saudi Arabia or the price of cars or television sets from Japan may overshadow other concerns. But always, whether in business or in personal relations, understanding depends on communication between people, and communication depends first of all on language. One of the greatest obstacles to understanding is the fact that people in different parts of the world do not understand each other's speech. The great majority of people never even master a second language—not, at least, well enough for fluent interchange of ideas. Misunderstandings are frequent enough when people speak the same language; it is much more difficult when they do not. There seems to be a universal tendency, even today, to look with suspicion on someone who is speaking a language that is strange to us. We wonder what that person is talking about, and it is easy to think he is saying something unpleasant about us.

Translations from one language to another are, of course, helpful, but they can cause trouble too. What is an idle figure of speech in one language can be a deep insult in another. In 1963, President Kennedy toured Europe, giving speeches wherever he went. He had prepared some practically foolproof jokes to tell, with the idea that laughter helps people to relax, and then they will listen to whatever is said next. But in Germany the jokes fell flat; no one laughed. What went wrong? Kennedy's interpreter did not know German quite well enough, and the points of the jokes were lost in translation. More recently Jimmy Carter had trouble in Poland because of poor translations.

It is language, no matter which one we speak, that makes the greatest difference between us and animals. We are born knowing how to use language; it is hard to imagine our lives without it. Anything that interferes with our effective use of language, whether it is inability to hear, to read, or—worst of all—to speak, becomes a serious handicap.

No one knows how language actually began. Sign language, gestures made by the hands, probably came first. Most scholars think that spoken language was a later development. But as to how it happened, there are almost as many theories as there are experts. One theory holds that spoken language grew mainly out of the cries and calls of animals. Early people first imitated animal sounds, then came to use the imitation to mean the thing itself. According to this theory—the "Bow-Wow" theory—"arrf-arrf" would mean dog, "oink" a wild boar, and so on.

Then there's the "Pooh-Pooh" theory, based on the probability that people made certain noises in certain situations. Life was rough and uncomfortable in those days, and a person might often stub a toe on a rock or prick a finger with a sharp thorn. "Ow!" he would exclaim. A hunter, charged by a dangerous animal, might have cried out, "Aggh-aggh! O! Wow!"

The "Ding-Dong" theory holds that people may have imitated other natural sounds they heard around them: "Whoo" for the wind, "Boom-Boom!" for thunder. Or perhaps people sang or chanted together as they worked, hauling home the meat from a slain mastodon or chipping away at stone to make tools, and certain human sounds came to be associated with certain activities. "Yo-He-Ho" is this theory's happy name.

People probably danced and sang before they made everyday use of language. We can imagine their song of joy when they were successful in the hunt and had brought home meat enough for everyone. The gestures that went with the song became a dance. Gestures in fact must have accompanied all the sounds that people made, for pointing fingers and sweeping motions of the arms could vividly express ideas. A gentle touch could convey affection. The meaning of a swift kick was no doubt as clear then as it would be today.

Many years must have passed before these sounds and gestures became language. To communicate in an intelligible fashion, day by day, people must adopt a definite set of spoken sounds and agree on their meaning. In the same way, gestures can become a sign language, like that used today by the deaf.

People made pictures long before they had any kind of writing. The first ones were for magic. It was thought that a picture drawn or painted on the wall of a cave might help a hunter to catch the animal that was represented by placating its spirit. This was important, because killing an animal meant food for the hunter and his family.

The earliest paintings were not intended for communication between people but were a way of sending messages to the spirits that were thought to dwell in all the natural world. Later, pictures were used to tell stories or to record a great event—for instance, a flood in which many people were drowned.

Pictures that are used to tell a story or to convey a message are called pictographs. *Picto* means "picture." *Graph* is from an ancient Greek word meaning "writing." Pictographs are simplified pictures of actual things. As a way of communicating, they have serious limitations, because the drawing of an object may mean different things to different people. A circle, for instance, could mean the sun or the moon, or even the human eye. A few rays drawn around it would make it look more like the sun—or perhaps the moon? A dot in the center might make the circle suggest an eye, but this was in fact the Egyptian hieroglyph for sun: ⊙   As with any writing, pictographs can get a message across only when their meaning is already known to a number of people.

Besides, there are a great many things which you cannot make a picture of at all. How would you draw happiness? You might make a picture of a smiling face, but there are many kinds of smiles, and your meaning would still not be clear. How about a picture of love? Well, that you can do, you say, and you draw a picture of a heart: ♡

This "heart shape" has, to be sure, become a generally accepted symbol for *love*. But it represents an idea or a feeling, not a thing. Such signs are called ideographs—that is, "idea writings." Sometimes, as time went on, the same sign could be used both as a pictograph and an ideograph. The Egyptian hieroglyph for *sun*, a pictograph: ⊙ , could also mean *day*, the time when the sun shone. You cannot see the day or make a picture of it, but a pictograph of the sun gives you the idea, and so it becomes an ideograph.

Another example. The Egyptian hieroglyph for *star* was easy to grasp: ⋇ . Sometimes, however, this stood for just the star of dawn; as such, it was still a pictograph. But it could also be an ideograph meaning "prayer." Egyptians often prayed in the early morning, when they could see in the sky only a few stars of dawn.

Writing of any kind came much later than spoken language and followed naturally the telling of stories in pictures. It was developed by different people in different places, somewhere between 5,000 and 10,000 years ago. Writing was—and still is—an invented system of visual marks used for communication among people. Of course, only those who knew the meaning of these marks, or signs, could communicate with them.

Curiously enough, the same signs, usually pictographs, sometimes developed in places quite far apart. The Egyptians and the Chinese, who could hardly have consulted each other,

had the same sign for the sun: ⊙. An American Indian pictograph for water ∿∿∿∿ was much the same as the Egyptian
hieroglyph ∿∿∿. This is easy to understand; it *looks* like
moving water.

There are many differences between sign making and
modern writing. For one thing, pictographs and ideographs
have no connection with the sounds of any spoken language.
This is an important difference. A person who wanted to learn
writing would, in effect, have to learn a whole new language.
This is no doubt one reason why relatively few people in
ancient times ever did learn to write. In Egypt only the scribes
mastered the thousands of hieroglyphs that made up their
writing. (The word *hieroglyph* comes from two ancient Greek
words meaning "sacred carving.") The ability to write gave the
scribes great power. They did not want other people to learn
and so resisted, for many years, any attempt to simplify the
writing.

The American Indians, on the other hand, had a very clear
and simple picture writing that was intended to get a message
across to as many people as possible. This writing, also not
associated with the sound of words, was in use until quite
recently.

In time writing was developed in which signs, or combinations of signs, represented the sounds of spoken syllables.
These could be combined to indicate words. Egyptian hiero-
glyphic writing had a number of such signs. Having more of
them would have made the Egyptian writing easier to learn.

The letters of our own alphabet represent the sounds that
make up our spoken words. This alphabet has a long history,
dating back to the ancient Semites, who worked for Egyptians
and adapted certain Egyptian sound-signs for their own use in
keeping records. Almost 3,000 years ago, the Phoenicians, who
lived near the Semites on the shores of the Mediterranean Sea,
in turn adapted the Semitic system to create their own writing.
The Greeks made further changes and added vowels, which
had not been thought of before, and made the written language
much easier to read. The Romans, west of the Greeks on the
Mediterranean, changed the Greek alphabet still more. We are

using the Roman alphabet today, two thousand years later. It is the most widely used of all the alphabets in the world, and there are now about fifty. The twenty-six letters of our alphabet can be used over and over again in different combinations to represent a practically unlimited number of spoken words. No more efficient method of writing has ever been invented.

Still, written signs or symbols can express some ideas better than phonetic alphabets, even today. The best-known signs that are used all over the world are our numerals, ten of them: 1 2 3 4 5 6 7 8 9 0. Differences in language make things complicated enough, but it would be almost impossible for business people to buy and sell if they could not read each other's written numbers.

Actually, our system of numerals is not the only one in the world. The Chinese and the Japanese, and followers of Islam in the Middle East and parts of Asia and Africa, have their own numerals. But our system, which is called Arabic, but which came originally from the Hindus of India, is almost universally understood.

You can probably think of other written or printed signs that are in use today. International road signs. Musical notations. Punctuation marks. Mathematical signs. Information signs on maps. Signs used by scientists. All these are important because they can be understood by people who speak different languages. In their own way they help us to realize that we live in one world.

Traditional Chinese writing, still in use today, consists of thousands of characters that were derived from early pictographs and ideographs. This is difficult for anyone, even the Chinese, to learn to write or read. In recent years the Chinese have devised simplified characters and even a phonetic alphabet similar to ours, so that more people can learn to read and write.

There is one great advantage in a written system that is not based on a spoken language—people of many different tongues can use it to communicate. This has been especially important to the Chinese, whose spoken language is broken up into numerous very different dialects. Chinese who could not understand each other's speech could at least understand each other through the written language, and this has been an important unifying force.

Today we have Blissymbolics, a system of graphic symbols logically designed for the express purpose of making it possible for people to communicate across language barriers. Blissymbolics is much simpler than Chinese writing. You will see how its logic and simplicity have opened doors to handicapped people all over the world.

·2·

Across Language Barriers

In the book of Genesis, eleventh chapter, we read of the Tower of Babel. "And the whole earth was of one language," the story begins. The descendants of Noah, speaking all one language, journeyed from the east and decided to build a city on a plain in the land of Shinar. In this city they wanted to raise a tower whose top would reach to heaven. Their purpose was to make a name for themselves, so they would be remembered in future times even if they and their descendants were scattered "upon the face of the whole earth." The Lord came down and saw the people building this tower and he did not like it. They were presumptuous, he thought, to attempt such a thing, for if they could do this, then nothing would be impossible for them. It was not right for mere humans to have so much power.

The Lord's way of dealing with this was to confuse the language of these people so that they no longer understood one another's speech. In this state of confusion they could not finish building their tower, and the Lord indeed scattered them "upon the face of all the earth."

The city was called Babel, and this word has come to mean confusion of any sort, whether related to language or not.

Differences in language have continued to plague the people of the world, creating misunderstanding and confusion everywhere. This is most obvious in spoken languages, but it is equally true of written or printed words. Most writing, like ours, is phonetic; the letters, or combinations of letters, represent sounds. To understand such writing, you have to know the spoken language that is represented. If your language is English, you can read English words written with the letters of our alphabet. But French words written with the same alphabet would mean nothing to you, unless you had learned French as a second language.

Surely something can be done about this—someone could invent a really practical way for people to communicate across language barriers. Many people have tried. In the past three hundred years, there have been more than two hundred attempts to invent a single spoken and written language for international use. Until about 1600, Latin was the nearest thing to an international language; every educated European could speak and write Latin. But it had some of the faults of any other language that had developed spontaneously over the years: some of its words meant different things to different people. What was wanted was a clear and simple language in which each word would mean the same thing to everyone, whatever his race or nationality. It is not surprising that no one achieved this. One of the difficulties was that a language that seemed altogether logical to its inventor might seem wildly fanciful to other people. None of the invented languages was simple enough.

In the seventeenth century the famous mathematician and philosopher Gottfried Wilhelm von Leibnitz had a dream; he could see clearly the need for a universal written language that would be, he said, "an algebra of thought." Chinese writing fascinated him, but he felt that the characters were too complicated for international use. Universal writing, he said, should consist as far as possible of easily understood pictorial symbols—basically pictographs.

A Universal Symbolism [he wrote in 1679], very popular, might be introduced if small figures were employed in the place of words, which would represent visible things by their lines. . . . This would be of service for easy communication with distant nations, but if introduced also among us, without however renouncing ordinary writing, would be useful in producing thoughts less absurd and verbal than we now have. . . . I think these thoughts will someday be carried out, so natural appears to me this writing for increasing the perfection of our mind.

Pictorial symbols—these would make the difference. Earlier attempts at a universal language had employed abstract figures, not derived in any way from real objects. They were confusing.

Leibnitz did not carry out his idea of a language based on pictorial symbols, but he was sure it could be done.

Interest in new languages then waned considerably until the midnineteenth century. At that time languages appeared called Lingualumina, Kosmos, Communia, Chabe Abane, Alwato, Latinesce, and so on and on. These were all languages that could be spoken as well as written. The first really successful manufactured language, based mainly on English words, was called Volapük (a word derived from *world* and *speak*). It was presented to the world in 1879 by a German Roman Catholic priest. His book about it, *Grammar of the Universal Language for All Earthlings,* was translated into some two dozen other languages. Nevertheless, Volapük was really a very complicated and impractical language. It could have been improved, but its inventor refused to consider any changes in "his" language. The success of Volapük is a mystery; in any case its heyday was brief.

Esperanto has done better. This invented language was introduced in 1887, when Volapük was still popular, by a Pole named Ludovic Zamenhof, whose pen name was Dr. Esperanto, meaning Dr. Hopeful. Esperanto uses most of the letters of our alphabet and basic words from the leading languages of Europe. Its proponents claim that it is easier to learn than any natural language, and in fact it is the only such language that is now widely spoken.

As an example, here is the first verse of the Twenty-Third Psalm, in English and in Esperanto:

The Lord is my shepherd;
I shall not want.

La Eternulo estas mia paŝtisto;
mi mankon ne havas.

A Universal Congress of Esperanto has been held every year since 1905, except during World Wars I and II. The language is taught in schools scattered throughout the world and in some universities. Poetry has been written in Esperanto; so have novels and plays. Students correspond with other students who speak different languages. Scientists can cooperate in their research because they can read each other's reports. Though Esperanto is most widely spoken in western Europe, it has clearly played a significant part in international cooperation. People who speak Esperanto wear a little green star in the lapel or on the collar so that other people who know the language can recognize them and start to talk.

Isn't this, then, the final word in universal languages? Not quite. Though the users of Esperanto are scattered throughout the world, it is far from being accepted for general use. It remains an artificial language, foreign to all nations, and it is by no means as easy to learn as its backers claim. Probably only about a half million people are actually capable of making practical use of Esperanto. In any case, people are inclined to cherish the mother tongue they were brought up with and to look askance at other languages, even those that have been in use for thousands of years. It is even harder for people to accept a "made" language that has all too brief a history. A manufactured language simply does not possess the delicate shades of meaning, the depth of feeling, the charming idiosyncrasies that belong to a language that has grown as people used it in their work and play and in carrying on the business of the world.

Still, new attempts at universal languages have continued. Ido was a revised and simplified form of Esperanto. Then there were Ro, Nepo, Tutonish, Perfekt, Timerio, and many others.

The inventor of an abstract symbolic writing called Safo conceived the idea of a universal language during World War II when he was in contact with prisoners of war from a number of different countries. These men were living together but could not speak with one another; their only communication was gestures. The need for an international system of writing and speaking was obvious. Safo is abstract writing joined with a system of spoken syllables.

Interlingua has proved useful in the fields of medicine and science. Basic English was first constructed with a vocabulary of 850 English words. Special groups of words were added as they were needed, however, until now there are about 8,000. Lincos is so designed that it can be sent by radio or laser beam to faraway planets.

Why not, after all, just choose one existing language and teach it to young children from the very beginning, all over the world? Or choose a combination of languages? English, Spanish, and French are already widely used in the Western world. A good idea, if the language could be properly standardized so that everyone could be sure of the meanings of words. But it seems unlikely that this will be done in the near future.

None of this is what Leibnitz had in mind. As we have seen, he visualized a pictorial written language, not based on the sounds of spoken words, that would be learned by everyone in his youth. Someone would first have to create a really practical system of pictorial symbols. And this brings us to the story of Charles Bliss and his Blissymbolics.

·3·

Charles Bliss and His International Symbols

Charles Bliss was convinced that people everywhere needed, above all, a system of symbols that could be used for communication across language barriers. Nothing else, he was sure, could do more to bring peace to our troubled world. And he himself would be the one to create these symbols and fulfill at last Leibnitz's dream of uniting mankind through symbols.

Bliss, whose name was then Karl Blitz, was born in 1897 in Austria-Hungary, near the Russian border. There, as he says, ten different nationalities "hated each other because they thought and spoke in different languages." As a boy he heard people speaking Ukrainian, Romanian, Polish, Russian, Yiddish, and German. He himself first learned German, the language of his mother and of the Austrian authorities. Young Karl puzzled a great deal about the confusion caused by differences in language. He could not understand, for example, why the life-giving liquid called *Wasser* (in German) should also be called *water, agua, aqua, eau, voda,* and so on. He soon found that there was no such confusion in the chemical formula for water; it is H_2O in all languages, and these symbols show the elements that water is made up of. It seems logical that Bliss became a chemical engineer, a very successful one. He never gave up his ambition to help people understand each other in spite of differences in language, though as yet he had no idea where this ambition would lead him.

15

Then Hitler came to power, and in 1938 his troops occupied Austria. Karl Blitz, a Jew, was sent to Dachau and later to Buchenwald. In these concentration camps, he found that the only language that was understood by everyone was music. He charmed even some of his jailers by playing a mandolin and guitar and actually managed to secure his own release. He fled first to England, where he changed his name, and then made his way to Shanghai, China, where his wife joined him on Christmas Eve, 1940.

In Shanghai Bliss became fascinated by Chinese writing, which, as we have seen, is made up of characters based on early pictographs and ideographs. It is a difficult writing to learn, because there are so many characters. But it did make it possible for people who spoke different dialects to communicate, once they had mastered the writing. This is what impressed Bliss.

Nothing fazed Bliss. He studied Chinese, and soon, although he could not speak a word in any Chinese dialect, he could read headlines in Chinese newspapers. As he deciphered the characters, he sounded out their meaning in German or English. A Frenchman would have read them in French, a Russian in Russian.

This, then, was to be Charles Bliss's way of helping humanity. He would develop a workable system of pictorial symbols, not based on the sound of spoken words. The symbols would be much simpler than the Chinese characters and so clear and logical that anyone could learn them. He started working on his symbols in 1942. After World War II, he and his wife emigrated to Australia. There, in Sydney, he earned his living at first on an automobile assembly line. But his real work was his symbols, and he never forgot that.

At last, in 1949, Bliss finished his great work, three volumes in manuscript form, which he titled *Semantography* (from the Greek words for "meaning" and "to write"). Leibnitz would have approved.

The next step was to spread the news. A logical symbol system that could express almost any meaning had at last been created—surely people everywhere would welcome it. But new ideas are often not appreciated by the very people who would benefit most from them. Bliss's wife, Claire, sent out 6,000 letters to educators, scholars, and experts on language, explaining clearly just what Bliss had accomplished and including examples of his symbols. A few important people responded, praising Bliss's work. The great biologist Julian Huxley said, "Bliss's work provides something of real importance," and the famous mathematician and philosopher Bertrand Russell wrote, "I think very highly of Bliss' work. . . . The symbols are ingenious and easy to understand, and the whole is capable of being very useful . . . an important service to mankind." But most of the letters went unanswered.

This was far from the enthusiastic acceptance Bliss had hoped for. In Australia, his adopted country, his work was at first completely ignored, and the disappointment was too much for Claire. She suffered a heart attack, and after eight years of ill health died in 1961. Bliss was desolate, but he continued his work on the symbols, and a revised one-volume edition of *Semantography* was published in 1965—882 pages. This time Bliss added the word "Blissymbolics" to the title of the book and to the name of the organization he had formed to publish his work: Semantography (Blissymbolics) Publications. He did this because the word "semantography," though it was Bliss's own invention, could be used as a regular English word. (After all, many English words are derived from the Greek.) In fact, some professors in universities were already talking about various "semantographies." Blissymbolics, on the other hand, was a word that could not be stolen because it contained Bliss's name.

About this time there was a greatly increased interest in signs and symbols in many parts of the world. One reason for this was the tourist explosion—more people were traveling than ever before. Under the leadership of the United Nations, a committee of experts devised a set of graphic designs for regulating road traffic anywhere in the world. Most countries have adopted these signs, and they have, in general, worked out very well. They are a kind of international language.

Bliss had his own symbols for road safety and all kinds of

travel. The experts could have saved themselves a good deal of trouble if they had adopted these instead of designing new ones. Why they did not was something Bliss could not understand. Besides road safety, he had symbols for use on planes, in hotels, on trains, for shipping, postal communication, and much more besides. But though his symbols were very practical, other designers kept on making their own. There was competition as to who could create the best signs for everyday use. The result was considerable confusion.

Bliss never doubted that eventually his symbols would be adopted. After all, he had created much more than road signs. The most complicated thoughts and feelings could be expressed with his symbols. And as he worked with the symbols day after day, Bliss began to see that they might also help people to think clearly. The symbols were new, and they made sense. The words in our spoken languages, on the other hand, have a long history of use and misuse. Many of them have gathered meanings and implications that modify the original meaning considerably. The results, though rich and subtle in expression, can be confusing as well. In some cases, even dangerous.

Nevertheless, it was never Bliss's intention that his symbols should replace alphabetical writing. We need the written form of our comfortable, eloquent mother tongues. But Blissymbolics gives us an extra tool to help us understand our world and the people in it. This in itself, he hoped, could help bring peace to the world.

Now for the general plan of Blissymbolics.

Whenever possible, Bliss made his symbols look like the things they represent. These are *pictographs*.

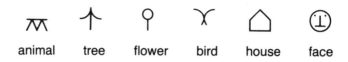

animal   tree   flower   bird   house   face

Some symbols are *ideographs;* they represent ideas in graphic form, showing how we think about our world.

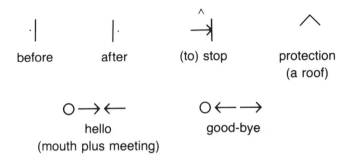

Bliss saw that the more pictorial a symbol can be, the clearer the meaning. That, he thought, must have been why Leibnitz insisted on pictorial symbols.

Some abstract symbols, however, are so familiar that everyone already knows their general meaning. These were included in Bliss's system with little change.

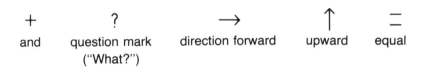

A few of the new symbols are arbitrary—that is, they were invented without reference to real things, simply because they were needed.

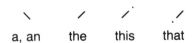

There are 100 basic symbol elements in Blissymbolics. These can be combined to make thousands of meanings.

man   and   protection   becomes   father

The symbols could be put on a specially constructed typewriter because each one consists of a combination of basic straight lines, angles, curves, and circles:

Learning to communicate with these symbols is not the same as learning to read. Actually, it is much easier, especially for people who have difficulty with hearing or seeing. A small child can learn symbols long before he knows how to read. An adult who has never learned to read can easily learn them, too. Of course, to communicate with any symbols, the meaning must be known both to the one who wants to "say" something and to the one who wants to understand. This problem has been solved in the use of Blissymbols by having the corresponding word (in whatever language) printed with each symbol. This makes it possible for a nonspeaking person to communicate with someone who can read but who does not know the meaning of the symbols, though a more varied conversation can take place if the speaking person does learn the symbols.

Most important of all, these symbols can be arranged to express complete sentences. Without that capability, communication has little meaning and degenerates into a disconnected series of isolated things and incomplete ideas.

I will come to see you.

These symbols will be explained more fully further on, but to

help clarify them a little right now, note that the symbol ⊥ means any *human being,* standing upright. The numbers 1 and

2 make this more specific. The small mark .... placed above the symbol for *come* makes it indicate action in the future. The

symbol ⊙ by itself means *eye;* the mark ᴧ .... over it changes it to an action symbol, meaning *to see.*

Another sentence:

Please   read

You can see that the symbol for *read* is a compound: *to see* plus a simple oblong meaning a *page* (of a book).

These sentences are two small examples to show you the beautiful flexibility of Blissymbols, which made it possible to extend the power of speech into areas where it had never been dreamed it could go.

·4·

Blissymbols in Toronto

There had to be a better way. Teachers at the Ontario Crippled Children's Centre in Toronto had been trying for years to find a way for young nonspeaking children to get their ideas across. They had used word boards and spelling boards and special electric typewriters with the older children, who could learn to read even though they could not speak. But these were no good with the younger children who could not yet read.

To be sure, pictures helped. At least some of the young children could point to a picture of a glass of water if they wanted a drink or a picture of their mother or father if they were lonely. But this was not nearly enough. For one thing, there are a great many things you cannot make pictures of—ideas, feelings, other intangibles. And besides, pointing at pictures is not the same as communicating with other people on a give-and-take basis. Young children normally share quite complicated ideas with each other and with adults long before they can read. Nonspeaking children cannot do this.

Shirley McNaughton, a teacher, and Margrit Beesley, occupational therapist, got together in 1971 and tried to work out something for these children. Since they couldn't draw pictures of thoughts and feelings, they decided they would have to make abstract symbols. With the help of a psychologist, a speech specialist, and a technician, they tried. The first design was a sort of abstract handshake to represent a greeting. They made other symbols and tried them out on the children. But it was hard, slow work, and discouraging.

Shirley McNaughton then began looking in libraries for books that might help. In the Toronto Library she found my book *Signs and Symbols Around the World.* Eight pages in it were devoted to Charles Bliss's Semantography. Excitedly Shirley McNaughton pored over them, discovering some of the symbols she and the others had been trying so hard to get ideas about—father, mother, child; and feelings—happiness, sadness. This could be it, she thought. She showed the book to the others, and they felt the same excitement.

They wrote to me, and I sent them a photocopy of Bliss's tourist folder with more symbols on it. Most of these were not suitable for the children, but the teachers tried out a few and found that the youngsters picked up each new symbol as fast as it was given to them.

Then they wrote to Charles Bliss in Australia, enclosing a captivating picture of Kari, who was one of the first "symbol children." Bliss had always hoped that his symbols would help humanity in some fashion, but he had never, even in his wildest imagination, foreseen what had happened in Toronto. He wrote back:

> I cannot express the emotion that swept over me when I held your letter and the picture of Kari in my hand. It was the finest present I ever got in my long life—now in its seventy-fifth year.
>
> For nearly thirty years, since I started my harebrained scheme of modern symbol-writing, I have thought of almost nothing else than applications for my symbols to help humanity. But never, never did it occur to me that they could help paralyzed children who cannot form words for thoughts or thoughts for words.

He gave the Ontario Crippled Children's Centre permission to go ahead with the use of his symbols. Enthusiastically, they did so, pioneering an astonishing breakthrough in human communication.

The story of how these symbols are being used with nonspeaking children—and adults—is an exciting one for anyone who is interested in helping people to develop the best possibilities that lie within them. Through using symbols, nonspeaking children—and adults, too—can communicate meaning directly, without reference to the sound of words. Many of the Blissymbols fit in perfectly with the children's experience. And there are so many possibilities, so much that can be "said."

Interest in Blissymbols soon spread beyond the Ontario Crippled Children's Centre, reaching George Lynes of the National Film Board of Canada. He himself had a young son who could not speak, and he knew how much it could mean to parents of such children to be able to communicate with them. Why not tell people about the symbols through a film? The result was *Mr. Symbol Man,* a remarkable film produced by the National Film Board of Canada and Film Australia. Charles Bliss is the hero of this documentary, and he is a real ham actor. He rolls around big white blocks with symbols on them, he juggles balls, he plays his mandolin. The children are there, Kari among them, their faces alive with the wonder of "saying" what is on their minds as they point to the symbols. It was a child who suggested the title of the film—by pointing:

Mr. Symbol Man

Toward the end of the film there is an animated cartoon sequence, created to help the children learn the symbols. In it lines dance around and form themselves into symbols. In turn, the symbols somehow come to look more like the things they are supposed to represent. An animal symbol really *is* a cat. People love this film.

In order to carry out the work of training teachers in the use of symbols, and to make sure the symbols are properly designed and used, an organization called the Blissymbolics Communication Foundation (later Institute) was formed in

Toronto in 1975. Charles Bliss signed an agreement with this organization, giving them permission to use his symbols and providing that he would act as a consultant to the foundation in the development of new symbols. He seemed happy with this arrangement.

As time went on, however, Mr. Bliss became less enthusiastic about the work of the institute. He could not seem to understand their point of view. After all, he had originally developed his symbol system for the purpose of international communication across language barriers, not for the use of the handicapped. For this reason, people who were working with nonspeaking children found it necessary, from the very first, to make certain changes in the symbols, in order to adapt them to the specific communication needs of these children. In order to work out these changes in cooperation with Mr. Bliss, which would involve considerable work on his part, people at the Blissymbolics Communication Institute agreed to pay substantial fees to Mr. Bliss's organization, the Semantography Trust of Australia.

By an agreement made with Mr. Bliss in 1976, when the B.C.I. finds it necessary to print a symbol in a form not approved by him, the sign Ⓑ is printed next to the symbol. The same is done with new symbols on which Mr. Bliss has not given advice or comment.

In the beginning mistakes were made. This was inevitable, since no one had ever done this particular kind of work with symbols before. With experience, however, the institute had worked out, by 1979, a standard form for over 1,400 symbols. Symbols designed by Mr. Bliss were kept in their original form whenever possible. His advice was sought on any changes or modifications that seemed necessary, and his suggestions or objections were carefully considered. As time went on, however, it became more and more difficult to get his cooperation in developing the new symbol vocabulary needed by the rapidly growing numbers of symbol users.

In spite of these difficulties, the Blissymbolics Communication Institute has continued its work of training teachers who want to use the symbols, providing teaching materials, and developing a standard symbol vocabulary. This has of course not been done in a vacuum. The important thing, always, has been what the symbols mean in the lives of nonspeaking people.

Who are the children who need the symbols? Most are victims of cerebral palsy, in which lack of muscle control is often (though not always) a symptom. Cerebral palsy is caused by damage to the brain, usually occurring at birth, although early-life injury and certain kinds of illness or poisoning can be causative agents as well. Cerebral palsy is not a disease; it is a condition, and there is no cure.

Cerebral palsy can be so mild that the only symptom is a slight difficulty in speaking. In severe cases, like Kari's, victims lack adequate control of the muscles that make their bodies move. Some of these children can walk with difficulty, others not at all. Most have limited control of head and hands. Their actions may appear jerky and uncertain. Often it is hard for them to hold on to anything with their hands or even to point with their fingers, and consequently most cannot write or draw or flash the deft signs by which the deaf communicate.

Actually, most children with cerebral palsy can speak, though not always clearly. Only about 8 or 9 percent of them cannot speak at all, but this amounts to thousands in North America alone. Most of these children can see and hear —some better than others—and they can feel. These functions do not require motor muscles. But the muscles of their throats and jaws either cannot form words at all, or the words come out in such a jumble that few people can understand them.

Just think, how does a child get an idea or feeling across if he cannot speak? He might want to say he is lonely or angry, or that he wants a drink of water or needs to go to the bathroom. He could perhaps nod his head, yes or no, or wave a hand this way or that. Some of the children cannot even do that. A few can indicate yes or no only by rolling their eyes one way or the other.

Young children normally explore their world by running from place to place, by poking into corners, by handling things to find out what they feel like, by talking, listening, looking. And they learn about themselves by practicing every possible motion and noticing how it feels and what happens as a result. This is how normal children find their way in the world of adults. But these physically handicapped children cannot run or poke into corners or handle things, and they cannot learn much from their very limited motions. If they also cannot speak, they are in real trouble. They are cut off from the give-and-take of ordinary conversation, from idle chitchat and asking "why" and exchanging ideas, one of the most important ways in which children grow in knowledge and understanding. Perhaps this is the worst deprivation of all.

In former times it was usually thought that all these children were retarded, simply because they could not communicate. No one supposed they could learn very much. Now we know that, though some are retarded, others are no more so than you or I. Besides, they can laugh and be happy or feel frustrated and angry like anyone else. They want to be loved, and they can give love in return. And they can learn.

Most of these nonspeaking children could *see* the world around them and the people in it—mother, father, brothers and sisters, teachers. Most could *hear* what was said to them and understand it. But this was, for them, a one-way street, their only possible response yes or no—like a lifelong game of Twenty Questions. Try going through a whole day saying nothing, only moving your head yes or no, no matter what is said to you, and you will see how frustrating this can be. No wonder the children often gave up and did not even try to learn.

The contact between nonspeaking children and the world was so slight and unsatisfactory that in time they often felt themselves to be as stupid as other people thought they were. As often happens, well-meaning people would often talk *at* the children, or *about* them in their presence, rather than *to* them, forgetting that they could hear and understand like anyone else. This did not help.

Today there are many ways of helping these children to communicate: word boards they can point at, spelling boards, various adaptations of electric typewriters, and now Blissymbols. By means of Blissymbolics, nonspeaking children can "talk" to their families and their teachers and friends. They can even ask questions.

Most children are used to asking questions; it's as natural as breathing. But these handicapped youngsters had never, in their whole lives, asked a single question, and many did not know how. Think of the many things a child would never find out if he could not ask "why" and "what's that." And he could never say to his mother, "Do you love me?" when he especially wanted to hear it.

Children who cannot speak must learn the practical details of everyday living in a different way from normal children, their exploration of their surroundings is so limited. They may find their way in a sort of hit-or-miss fashion; this can cause a great deal of confusion and unhappiness. It is better when a wise teacher guides them as they learn, one step at a time.

For the nonspeaking children in Toronto, learning to communicate with symbols meant a whole new way of thinking and feeling. New ideas, new possibilities stirred in their minds. It was like waking up from a long dim daydream. Children who had felt like nonpersons, sitting like lumps in wheelchairs, discovered that they were somebody after all.

One little girl, when she had learned to use the symbols, "asked" her parents, "Why are you not speaking to me?"

The father, who loved his little girl, suddenly realized that, because she could not respond, he hardly ever did speak to her. Now he could see that she was lonely and needed people to talk to her even if she could not talk back.

Until this time nobody had any idea what went on in the minds of these children. But, frustrated and locked up in silence though they were, they had been listening and watching and storing up thoughts and feelings. Once they were able to express themselves, this all came bursting out—sometimes with the force of an explosion.

When the project first started, about a dozen symbols were arranged in a semicircle on a tray fastened onto the wheelchair, above the child's lap. A pointer could be moved to indicate any symbol. That is the device that Kari is using in the picture taken when she was seven years old. Within a few weeks the number of symbols used by Kari had to be increased to thirty. Today a child (or sometimes an adult, as we shall see) may have more than 500 symbols before him, usually printed in squares on a rectangular board. The corresponding word is printed above each symbol, in English or whatever language the child and his parents are familiar with. Symbols may also be placed on the wall, on a board that folds up for easy carrying, or on a handkerchief a child can carry in his pocket. There are even T-shirts with symbols printed on them. Kari's mother put up symbols on cards around her kitchen so she could communicate with Kari while she worked.

The children point to the symbols they want to say, if they can. They may combine their pointing with gestures, vocal sounds, and whatever else they can manage to get their idea across. Children who cannot point with fingers or fists may point with their eyes, or they may use other means of indicating symbols—joy sticks, head sticks, electronic devices that can be operated by whatever part of the body is most usable. All this must be carefully adapted to the individual, as must the mode of instruction, which will be discussed in the next chapter.

·5·

Learning Blissymbols

There are many ways of learning Blissymbols. How a person learns them depends on his particular communication problem, how fast he can learn, how much or how little he can talk, and his age—even two-year-olds can learn some symbols.

Young children will probably work first with objects, then pictures, beginning with very simple ones. Concepts such as *yes* and *no* are learned by associating them with something the child cares about. (John wants a ball—yes!) Then the meanings are repeated, with examples, over and over again.

The first symbols learned are those that represent *things,* the pictographs. They are presented on cards, clearly written or printed, one at a time. Which ones are chosen depends on the interests of the individual child or adult. A ball for John. An animal for Susie. New shoes for Anne. The teacher keeps a careful record of how each child learns. When a child knows enough to "say" something, the teacher may write down his sayings day by day in a notebook. This is *his* book, a record of *his* thoughts and feelings.

On the following pages you will find one way of learning some of the basic symbols. This is planned so that you can learn to say something with symbols in a relatively short time. It is not likely, however, that symbols would be taught in just this way to a person who is handicapped by cerebral palsy, because you will be learning to read *and* write them.

Wooden symbol blocks for preschool children.

Styrofoam blocks for young symbol users.

Let's start with something familiar, the parts of your body:

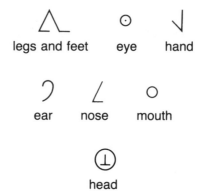

Each of these symbols, as you can see, is a simplified picture of the thing it represents. Blissymbols are designed this way whenever possible. If the symbol for hand seems puzzling, try holding your hand straight up, side view, with the thumb sticking out.

A symbol that represents a thing can often be changed to mean action by putting a little sign above it: .... This is called an action indicator, and it does not touch the symbol itself. Thus:

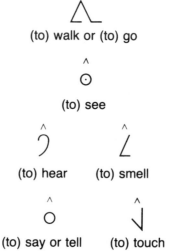

Now, by adding a few other symbols, we can make a sentence:

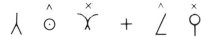

Man sees birds   and smells flowers.

Two of these symbols have a small × above them. This is another indicator, meaning plural. You have now learned two indicators—*action* and *plural*. The plural indicator is, after all, the familiar sign that means *multiply* in mathematics.

There is another mathematical sign in the above sentence, + for *and*. Blissymbolics also uses — for *minus*, ÷ for *division*, and the equal symbol, ⁼ These are some of the relatively few Blissymbols that are not based on real things.

Legs, eyes, ears, and so on are *parts* of the body. How about whole people?

The symbol for man came first in our sentence: ⋏

Here is the symbol for woman: ⋏

The first of these symbols represents a man in pants, and the second a woman in a skirt. But Charles Bliss had something additional in mind. The symbol for man, he says, has in it the

symbol for *action:* /\ This is always important for a man. Action can be important for a woman, too, but only a woman can bring a new human being into the world. So Mr. Bliss made the symbol for woman from the symbol for

creation: △ Actually, this symbol belongs not only to Bliss; it is a very old sign for *woman*.

Here is the symbol for *child* (boy or girl): ♀

It is a combination of *flower* ♀ and *little* ⊥

Little flower!

Blissymbolics

An adult, then, is a big flower: ♀

This is a combination of *flower* ♀ and *big* I

A teenager is somewhere in between ♀

You can probably figure out the reasons for the following yourself:

ጸ   ዪ   ᴏH

girl   boy   baby (cannot stand up yet)

The symbol ∧ means *male* in general; △ means female.

These symbols can refer to male or female people, dogs, cats, chickens—anything. (The male or female symbol is usually written after the symbol for the person or animal.)

The child's father is, of course, a man: ⅄

and his (or her) mother is a woman: △ Together they

are a married couple: ⅄△

—that is, a man and woman holding up a roof because a roof means the home where the family can feel safe and protected. And when a baby is born, it is as if a new star appeared under the roof.

So this is the symbol for birth: ⚹

And the husband and wife as parents: ⅄⚹△

Now, the separate symbol for father: ⋏

And for mother: △

Here the added lines at the top represent the arms of the mother or father reaching out to the child with love.

Now let's try another sentence:

/	⟁	+	⟁	❤	/	♀
The	mother	and	father	love	the	child.

In this sentence two new symbols have been added,

the symbol for *the*: ╱

and the symbol for (to) *love*:

(Note the action indicator over the symbol for *love*.)

This brings up the whole matter of symbols for feelings. These are, of course, not things you can touch or make pictures of. But throughout the ages a simplified drawing of a heart has been used to mean love and indeed any kind of friendly feeling toward another person. Blissymbolics uses the heart symbol as the basis for a whole collection of symbols for feelings.

The spoken words for feelings have nothing in common with one another. "Happy," "sad," "angry," "surprised"—these words, as we see them on a page, refer to spoken sounds, but there is nothing about their appearance to indicate that they share a common attribute—namely, they all express feelings. But Blissymbols are grouped together in appearance according to meaning. You can see this in the symbols for feelings:

joy, happiness—feeling going *up* ♡↑

sadness—feeling *down* ♡↓

much joy ✕♡↑   very much joy ✕✕♡↑

(The multiplication sign is used here again, but it is bigger than when it is used as an indicator *over* a symbol.)

✕✕♡↓	♡‼	♡‼!	♡↑o
despair	(to) surprise	excited	(to) laugh—

(Figure "to laugh" out yourself. The little ○ , if you remember, signifies the mouth.)

♡ +!   ♡ −!
(to) like   (to) dislike
                                 (the minus sign in mathematics.)

x ♡ ≪
anger
(much feeling in opposition)

You might try making up a sentence of your own, using the symbols you have learned so far. Draw them just as they appear in this book.

Perhaps you want to say *happy* or *sad,* instead of *happiness* or *sadness.* You can do this by using another indicator, a small

mark like this: .... placed over the symbol (again not touching it).

♡↑   ♡↓   x♡≪
happy   sad   angry

Bliss calls this indicator an *evaluator.* Symbols with this indicator on top represent adjectives or adverbs; they describe a thing or tell what somebody thinks it looks like or feels like.

Now you know three indicators, each one to be placed over a symbol to help us understand what it means:

the action indicator, to make a symbol
represent an action word, a *verb.*   ....

the plural indicator, formed from the
international symbol for multiplication.   ....

the description (evaluation) indicator, to
make a symbol represent an adjective or   ....
adverb.

You can say in symbols:

$$\underset{\text{I}}{\underset{1}{\bot}}\quad \underset{\text{am}}{\overset{\wedge}{\oplus}}\quad \underset{\text{happy.}}{\overset{\vee}{\heartsuit}\uparrow}$$

Or maybe instead you are feeling lonely:

$$\underset{\text{I}}{\underset{1}{\bot}}\quad \underset{\text{am}}{\overset{\wedge}{\oplus}}\quad \underset{\text{lonely.}}{\overset{\vee}{\heartsuit}-\bot}$$

This introduces another useful set of symbols:

$\bot$ means any human being. (We have seen this before. It represents a standing person, feet out to the side.)

Thus, the symbol for lonely $\overset{\vee}{\heartsuit}-\bot$ is a compound symbol meaning *feeling minus person*—feeling all alone because nobody's there.

$\underset{1}{\bot}$ means person number 1, *I,* or *me.*

$\bot 2$ person number 2, *you* (boy or girl, man or woman).

$\wedge 3$ means *he* or *him.*

$\triangle 3$ *she* or *her.*

Use the plural indicator to make we or us: $\overset{\times}{\bot}_1$

And *they* or *them:* $\overset{\times}{\bot} 3$

The symbol used above for *am* can also mean *is, are,* or (to)

be: $\overset{\wedge}{\oplus}$

This is made from the symbol for *life:*

which consists of the symbol for *sun:* and a modified form

of the symbol for *human being* or *person:*
(And the action indicator belongs above it because *being* is a kind of action.)

You will find that many of the symbols in Blissymbolics are compound. A few basic forms can be put together to make a great variety of meanings.

Before you start writing symbols, it would be a good idea to see exactly how they ought to be drawn. A symbol drawn one way may have a different meaning from the same symbol drawn smaller or placed differently on the page.

Blissymbols are constructed from a small number of basic shapes, drawn between two horizontal lines. The most accurate results can be achieved by using graph paper, ruled in squares.

Many shapes require a full square space, vertical and horizontal:

Some shapes occupy half a square space, vertical or horizontal:

Others only a quarter-square space, vertical or horizontal:

Bliss calls the bottom of the two horizontal lines the earthline and the top the skyline. A few symbols extend over the skyline or under the earthline. This gives the symbol a particular meaning.

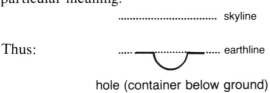

Thus:

hole (container below ground)

Indicators are placed a quarter space above the skyline.

Thus (to) feel

If you do not have graph paper handy, you might visualize each symbol within a square or part of a square.

The position and size of a symbol can change its meaning, Thus:

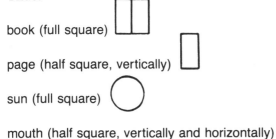

book (full square)

page (half square, vertically)

sun (full square)

mouth (half square, vertically and horizontally)

A full square separates symbols in a sentence.

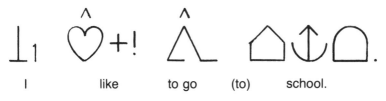

| I | like | to go | (to) | school. |

You will probably not want to go further than this into the drawing of symbols, but you can see by now that their meaning depends on accurate rendition of size, shape, and spacing.

A few more details about symbols. We have shown you the

action indicator ^ (to make verbs), the evaluation

indicator ^V (for adjectives or adverbs), and the plural

indicator. ^×

There is also a *thing* indicator: □ This is placed over a word (above the skyline) to make it mean a concrete *thing*— that is, something that can be handled, felt, or seen. The thing indicator is not needed when the symbol obviously indicates such a thing, but this is not always clear.

To show how indicators can change the meaning of a symbol:

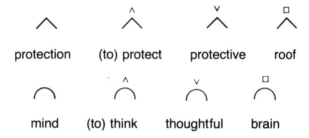

protection	(to) protect	protective	roof
mind	(to) think	thoughtful	brain

The action indicator creates the infinitive form of a verb or action in the present. For some symbol users that may be all they need to know about tense as an expression of time—more would be confusing. Others will want to know how to indicate future and past action.

Present tense, with action indicator: ⊥2 ^⟋⟍_
                You   walk (go)

Future action is indicated this way: ⊥2 ⟋⟍_
                You   will walk (will go)

And past action: ⊥2 ⟋⟍_
          You   walked (went)

Of course, most of the cerebral-palsied children cannot add indicators to symbols by drawing them, but displays have many symbols with the indicators already printed above them. For instance:

♡↑ ♡+!

happy (to) like

Moreover, indicators and other useful abstract symbols appear in separate squares on the display, and as the children master a larger vocabulary of symbols, they find that they can modify meanings by pointing to these special indicators as needed. (The indicator is pointed to first, then the symbol it belongs with.)

The pointer is a useful device. It is like the point of an arrow and it makes meanings more specific:

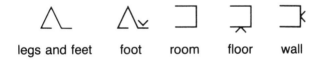

legs and feet   foot   room   floor   wall

The possessive symbol is equally useful: ...+...
For example:

⊥2+   ⊥3+

your, yours   their, theirs

Some symbol meanings depend on the position of dots or lines:

under   over   in, inside   out, outside

Some important words:

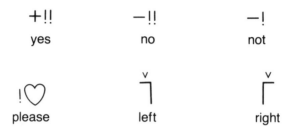

+!!	−!!	−!
yes	no	not

!♡	˅⏋	˅⎡
please	left	right

Arrows are used in intriguing ways:

hello	good-bye

You can figure those out, as well as these:

(to) turn	(to) jump	(to) mix

Numbers are sometimes used , as in the days of the week:

◯1	◯2	◯3
Sunday	Monday	Tuesday

Letters may be needed to make the meaning more specific:

⋀ d   ⋀ h

e.g., animal + letter = dog or donkey   horse

And how would you say Susie? Or Jim? You would have to write their names or initials. When I visited a class of nonspeaking children in Toronto, the children "wrote" about the visit, and I became

人H

(woman H for Helfman)

Later, I wrote in symbols to the children, and they replied in a letter that was composed by them and written down by their teacher, who included the English words. Here is their letter:

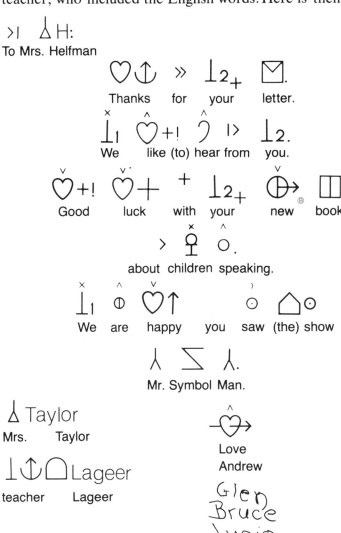

To Mrs. Helfman

Thanks for your letter.

We like (to) hear from you.

Good luck with your new book

about children speaking.

We are happy you saw (the) show

Mr. Symbol Man.

Mrs. Taylor

teacher Lageer

Love
Andrew

Glen
Bruce
Lucio
Susi
Ann R.

Children everywhere like to talk about food. Here is some symbol-talk from the school in Toronto.

I am hungry (feeling without food)

and thirsty. (feeling without drink)

I want milk (drink of life)

To eat I will have a hamburger (roll + food/animal = meat)

In the hall at the school there is a place where children's statements can be posted. They talk about what they like and don't like:

Laura says, I like the food.

Other food words:

ham (food/animal H)

cheese

lettuce (leafy vegetable)

See what messages you can write in Blissymbols. The small glossary of symbols at the back of this book will help you. If some symbols you want are missing, try making your own.

You may find this more difficult than you expect. It is quite different, for instance, from inventing signs for a secret code. The purpose of a secret code is to hide ideas; symbols should make ideas or information as clear as possible. You will find, as do the children who cannot speak, that "symbols do what talking does."

·6·

The Children and
Their Symbols

Timothy was discouraged. For all of his nine years, he had spent most of his waking hours in a wheelchair. He could not even sit up without a strap to hold him against the back of the chair, and although there was a head rest, his head kept falling over to one side. Sometimes he drooled. The worst was that he could not speak. It was frustrating never to be able to say anything to anyone, when there was so much going on in his head.

To be sure, good things had happened to Timothy—trips to the country, loving care from his family, and school at the Ontario Crippled Children's Centre in Toronto, where he was learning Blissymbols. There were other children like himself at school, and many times this helped Timothy at least to feel he was not alone. But on this particular day in spring he did feel alone.

He arrived at school in the special bus that transported the children. One wheelchair after another moved up the ramp to the door of the school, down the hallway, into the classroom. Some wheelchairs, including Timothy's, had to be pushed by someone. Other children could make theirs go by pushing a switch to activate a motor that turned the wheels. (Huge electric batteries rested on the shelf below the seat of the wheelchair.)

There were six boys and girls in Timothy's class. None of

A classroom display with symbols.

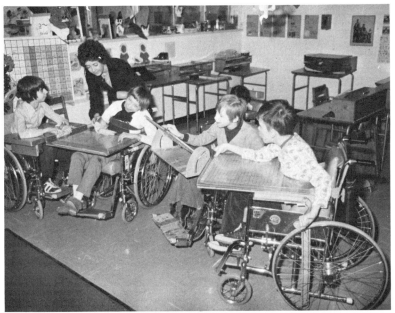

A classroom for symbol users.

them could speak. Each one had a board with 400 symbols on it attached to the front of his wheelchair, like a tray. Besides the teacher and her assistant, there were several trained volunteers to help, usually one adult for each child. The day began with a warm-up period, each child working with an adult, who wrote down in symbols whatever the child wanted to say. A skilled adult knows how to ask the right questions and how to help a child to find the right symbols, without ever telling him what to say. When the child is finished, he can *see* what is said, all written down in symbols.

Timothy could not point—his arms did not work well enough. His helper would point at symbols on his board, and he would wag his arms as best he could. One way meant "wrong symbol," the other way meant "that's it!" This was a difficult way to say anything and slow, but it worked better than you might think. Timothy's helper had been with him for some time, and she had a surprisingly good idea of what he might want to say. Timothy could feel that she loved him and really wanted to help.

This is what Timothy "said" to Sarah Jones, his helper, that morning.

I   am unhappy. Hands don't work.

Feet   don't work.

Only eyes work, ears work.

Some days Timothy might have had more to say, even though he did not as yet know many symbols. Not this time.

When the children had finished giving their messages to the adults who helped them, it was time to share them—if they wished. All six wheelchairs were turned so they faced the blackboard, and the teacher wrote their messages with white chalk. Any child could then ask questions or comment on what another child had said. This could get pretty lively sometimes.

Today Timothy was willing to share. The teacher copied his message onto the board from the notebook where Sarah Jones had written it. And this time Joyce, the girl who seemed to Timothy to know the most symbols, had an answer for him!

I had trouble too. Hands didn't work.

Feet didn't work. Only eyes worked,

ears worked. Now I have symbols.

I am very happy.

Timothy gave Joyce his best smile—a little crooked, but she knew what he meant.

The morning continued. There were symbols to learn or review, with the help of pictures, this time opposites: happy-sad, big-small, hot-cold, wet-dry. (Explanations of the "opposite" symbol come later in this chapter.)

Then there was a game in which the children figured out the right order of symbols in a scrambled sentence. After that Timothy was chosen to wave the Canadian flag while the teachers and helpers sang "O Canada," the Canadian national anthem. Timothy liked that. His flag waving was jerky and uncertain but full of enthusiasm.

These are only a few of the things that may happen on any

school day for these handicapped children. They try desperate-ly hard. Doggedly, step by step, they learn to cope with their inadequate bodies and to master the art of communicating with other people. Everything they do is slow, slow, slow, but this in itself does not bother the children. They have never done things any other way. It's only when adults expect them to act quickly that they discover that their way of doing things may not be the best way after all. Until they learn to com-municate, the brightest children are the most frustrated. So much goes on in their minds, unspoken, unshared. It is a lonely world.

Once they learn symbols, these children tease each other and play jokes, like any children. When Mr. Bliss was working on the film *Mr. Symbol Man* with Kari, she got him all confused by pointing to symbols that did not make sense. What was this? he wondered. And then it dawned on him that Kari was just playing a joke.

Darlene and Kari share some news.

Of course school is not all learning symbols. There is lunch, physical therapy, training in the use of the senses, and, in time, reading and other school subjects. And trips, to get acquainted with the larger world outside.

Life may be harder for these children when they are older. As adolescents they may realize only too well how much of life is passing them by, and they may become very depressed. Now there are good days and bad days, but even Timothy can often enjoy his school and his family.

The children in Timothy's class all used the same or similar symbol boards, a standard set of 400 symbols that was developed for their use. The earliest symbol arrangement, as we have seen, was a semicircle with a pointer that swung around to point at the desired symbol. This was easy to operate and it is still used at times, but it did not provide space for enough symbols. So rectangular boards of 100, 200, and 400 symbols were developed, with symbols arranged according to meaning—action words together, things of various kinds, descriptive words, adverbs, and so on. These boards could be fastened to wheelchairs and were often covered with plastic to protect them. Sometimes the boards were made to fold up. A child who could walk might even have had a small board hanging from his belt by an elastic.

Ideally each child should have a display that includes symbols for his own special needs and interests. This was always done when the child first began to learn symbols. But when it came to learning more, perhaps hundreds, a standard symbol board seemed the best solution. It would be just too difficult to design and print a separate selection for each child.

Then, in 1978, the Blissymbolics Communication Institute issued its symbol stamps. These are printed paper squares with self-sticking backs, one for each symbol. Grids are supplied that can be used for 100 to 512 symbols; these are printed smaller for the grid with more symbols. A guide to using the stamps is provided; it gives suggestions for organizing and applying the stamps, color coding, and so on. There are sample displays for beginning, intermediate, and advanced students.

Five-year-old Shantrell points to symbols.

Some of these samples are the standard displays that were developed earlier; a teacher may find one of these just what a particular student needs. A grid can also be cut to suit the physical capabilities of the user.

The use of stamps in varied arrangements has become the preferred way of presenting symbols to a nonspeaking person. This is much better than always using a standardized board that may not suit a particular individual at all.

This little man was invented to go with the symbol stamps. He is made up of symbols for various parts of the body and occupies two squares across and three squares down.

Learning symbols can be hard work. At one time Ann, a girl in Timothy's class, spent a good deal of time in a separate room, getting special instruction in symbols, while various electronic devices were tried. Ann is a practical child, and when she was finished, she wanted to say, "In the downstairs room where I work, I should be paid eight cents; it is difficult work." She did not have on her board all the symbols she needed to express the complete message, but she did the best she could:

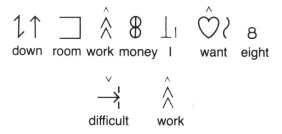

A word about some of these symbols. The *down* symbol is a combination, the opposite meaning of *up* (more about opposite meanings in the next part of this chapter). *Work* consists of two small action symbols and an action indicator. Ann wanted the noun but had only the verb form on her display. *Money* is the Mercury trade symbol from ancient Rome, simplified. (Mercury was the messenger of the gods.) *Want* is the heart symbol for feeling, with the symbol for *fire*. The symbol for *difficult* shows an arrow having a hard time trying to break through a barrier. (That's how Bliss conceived of this particular symbol, but it might be learned and remembered as if it were purely abstract.)

When I visited this class in the school at the Ontario Crippled Children's Centre a second time, after several months away, Ann looked very excited and indicated to her helper that she had something to say. This was her message:

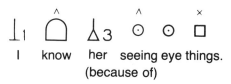

She remembered me because I wear eyeglasses—as she does. There was no symbol for glasses on her symbol board, but she got the idea across just the same. And her next message was:

$$\underset{\text{I}}{\perp}_{\text{I}} \quad \overset{\wedge}{\heartsuit}\text{+!} \quad \underset{}{\perp}_2$$

I   like   you.

Of course no board with 100, 200, or even 400 or more symbols on it can provide enough symbols to say *everything*. Ann found that out. The children have ways of overcoming this limitation through the use of special symbols. A new meaning can be created by combining a special symbol with an existing symbol. This is how it works:

Suppose Roberta wants to tell her mother she has a cold. There is no symbol for *cold* on her board, but that does not stop Roberta. She points to $\overset{\wedge}{\perp}_{\text{I}}$ (I), $\pm$ (have), then to $\overset{1}{\downarrow}$, (the symbol that indicates *opposite meaning*), and then to $\langle\langle\rangle\rangle$ (the symbol for *hot*).

Written or printed, the total result would look like this:

$$\underset{\text{I}}{\perp}_{\text{I}} \quad \pm \quad \overset{\vee}{\downarrow}\langle\langle\rangle\rangle$$

I   have [a] cold.

The opposite of *hot* is *cold*. The symbol for *cold* was left off the board simply to save space. This has been done also with other opposite meanings. For example, *big* is on the board, but not *little*. *Little* can be indicated by the symbols for *opposite meaning* and *big:*

$$\downarrow\overset{\vee}{\text{I}}$$

It is the same with *young* and *old:* $\downarrow\overset{\vee}{\text{Q}}$

Opposite meaning plus *young* means *old*. (A special symbol, when it is written or printed, is ordinarily placed one quarter space before the symbol with which it is used.)

The symbol for *part (of)* ÷ is another device that saves space on the board:

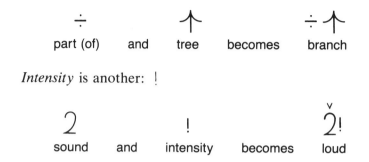

| part (of) | and | tree | becomes | branch |

Intensity is another: !

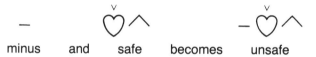

| sound | and | intensity | becomes | loud |

(Note that the *intensity* symbol is placed *after,* not *before,* the symbol it is used with.)

The symbol for *minus, without,* can also be used as a special symbol to create negative meanings:

| minus | and | safe | becomes | unsafe |

Most important for the children is the *combine indicator:* By using this, anyone can combine several symbols in his own way in order to say almost anything. This special symbol is placed before *and* after the symbols that are combined, just over the skyline. (You can see that it is important to know where the combination ends.)

George one day wanted to ask if the class could go on a picnic. No symbol for that. So he pointed to:

| combine indicator | food | outside | combine indicator |

Picnic!

Another problem: how to "say" *witch* on Halloween. Not impossible:

woman + make-believe + [like a] bird + sky

Witch—make-believe woman who flies in the sky!
Here are more combinations thought up by children.
Timothy wanted to say something about a *thermometer:*

thing (to) measure hot

And a *wallet:*

container for money

Rocco, who was about to move from an apartment to a house, wanted to talk about his family's new *refrigerator:*

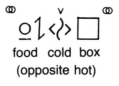

food   cold   box
(opposite hot)

(The first example of a combined symbol, meaning *picnic,* is spaced as separate symbols that the child would indicate on his display. The rest are properly spaced as symbols combined to achieve one meaning.)

The order of symbols is not always the same as the order of words in a spoken sentence. This is often made necessary by

the logic of the symbols themselves, and sometimes in combinations the order gets mixed up as the children struggle to get
their meaning across. This is all right. It is more important for a
child to say what he means than to duplicate English word
order.

Kari was especially good at thinking up combinations. One
day she *had* to tell her mother she had a problem. No such
symbol, but that didn't stop Kari. She pointed to:

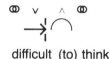

difficult (to) think

She used this combination often after that.

Silvano wanted to say he lived in an apartment. He made a
combination to mean *apartment:*

house in many houses

Silvano's symbol was so logical that it became, with only a
minor change, the standard symbol for apartment:

By observing how a child combines symbols, a teacher can
learn a great deal about how his mind works and how he
perceives the world. The combinations are, in fact, a very
personal matter, varying with the individual and serving the
needs of the moment. As long as the user gets his idea across,
no one minds if he uses the symbols in an offbeat way. But
these odd combinations will probably not become part of
accepted symbol usage, as Silvano's *apartment* combination
did. In this they differ from *compound* symbols, which are
standardized and were part of Bliss's original plan.

One more story about a symbol combination, this time

invented by a boy named Joe. He could talk, but not clearly, so he used symbols to supplement his speech when he got into difficulties. One time Joe was trying to tell his mother that he had had a big argument with his friend Wayne. The word "argument" came out all mixed up, and although Joe said it several times, his mother couldn't get it. So he turned to his symbol board. There was no symbol for *argument*—but never mind. Joe pointed to the symbols for *fight with words*. His mother could understand that:

fight with words
(hand crossing hand)   (part of + language, made up of mouth and ear)

Joe's speech actually became clearer after he started to use symbols. The pressure was off. He didn't have to worry about saying what he wanted to, because the symbol board helped him say almost anything.

There ought to be a book about the symbol children, written not for teachers but for the children themselves. So thought Shirley McNaughton, who helped start the symbol program in Toronto and is now Director of the Blissymbolics Communication Service. Mrs. McNaughton wrote the book herself, and the Ontario Crippled Children's Centre published it in 1975. It is illustrated with drawings of the children.

> Have you ever wondered [the book begins],
> How you would feel
> If only one person
> In the whole world
> Could understand what you were saying?
> Or—if not a single person could understand you?

You might think that you would feel

upset   or   angry   or   lonely

or that you would just want to stop thinking.

This is a story about children who know
how it feels not to be understood.
They have never been able
to speak clearly!
But they are

happy   and   excited

They do not feel ♡↑↓ or ♡−⊥ or ×♡≪.

They do not want to →| ∩ .
They have learned to talk in a new way!
Without even needing their mouths!

They talk with symbols: ⟍

It's time to "listen" with your eyes!

The rest of the book is narrated by John, one of the symbol
children. He tells a secret of each of the symbol children.

Kari's secret ☐ is women's lib:

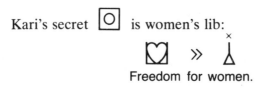

Freedom for women.

At the end of the book John says that the symbols are "from

us to ⊥2   Now—how does that make ⊥2 ♡ ?"

Symbols mean not only that nonspeaking children can reach out and express their pent-up feelings and ideas, but also that speaking people can enter into their world. They can know the feelings of these children, answer their questions, and respond to their need for love. To the children the most important part of their sharing is to know that someone else u iderstands and cares.

·7·

There Are Many Ways
of Learning

The children point to symbols if they can. This is the best way, but it is not as easy as you might think. It may involve moving a hand—or sometimes a toe—slowly and deliberately toward the symbol board, with one finger or toe outstretched, hoping that it will hit the right square the first time. Practice helps, and determination. The children have plenty of time. If someone told a child who was struggling to point to hurry, the pointing finger might go skittering off in the wrong direction. Some children cannot even extend a finger; they can only "fist point." This can be accurate enough, if the symbols on the board are not too small and the pointing is done with a knuckle or a finger joint.

For those who cannot point at all, there are electronic devices. An electric switch may be pushed or pulled to make a light go on under one square of a transparent symbol display. One such device is the Bliss scanner. When a switch is pushed, a light goes on and moves vertically downward on the left side of the display. Taking the finger off the switch when the light is at any point makes the light stop moving vertically and go horizontally instead, across the display. When a light reaches the desired symbol, taking the finger off the switch will make the light stay there until the switch is pushed again. Various switches are available, some of them responding to a very light touch.

I've used the word "finger" in describing how the scanner works, because that's what one would normally use to push a switch. But of course the important thing about this scanner is that it can be used by people who cannot point with a finger.

A great variety of switches is available for operating the scanner and other devices. Which one is chosen for a particular child depends on which part of his body he can use best. A joystick with a knob on top, for instance, may be pushed in two to eight directions. Perhaps the child's knee does the pushing. A foot trolley may be best for some children. And so on.

Does all this seem almost unbearably slow and cumbersome? That is not how it seems to these children. They are used to doing things slowly. And they know better than anyone else how much better this is than never being able to "say" anything at all. With practice, too, some children can operate these devices with surprising speed. A printer can be used to print, in a strip, the symbols that are indicated.

Peter is a ten-year-old child who cannot move any part of himself precisely except his head. Consequently, he uses a head stick, fastened to a band around his head and projecting out in

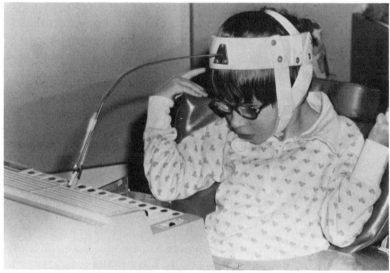

Ann plays the organ with a headstick.

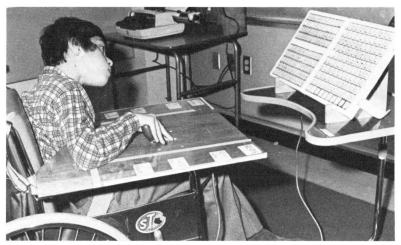

Silvano operates the Bliss scanner with a joystick.

front of him. By nodding his head vigorously, Peter can hit the square he wants on his symbol board. A magnet on the end of the stick activates a switch beneath the symbol, and it lights up. A printer then prints it. Peter had been thought to be retarded before he learned to use this device. He is not. He had just never been able to make any connection with the world around him. No retarded child could operate this device with the speed and precision that Peter is capable of.

Even Peter is one of the more fortunate ones. Some children must push a switch with their chin or even with mouth and tongue. A few can only roll their eyes to indicate yes or no when someone else points to a symbol.

If even the head stick doesn't work, there is the PMV scanner. On this device the letters of the alphabet are arranged in one horizontal line. Lights move across this row of letters and the child indicates the letter he wants by releasing the switch when that letter is lighted up. The scanner then prints it.

The devices used by these children may be just a beginning. Someday children may be able to feed information into a computer, and then the computer will draw symbols by following their instructions. This way a child could send a message to another child in another place—if he also had access to a computer.

All this is fairly complicated and very expensive, especially when we start thinking about computers. But there are much simpler devices that can help some children to feel at home in their world. One child who could walk wore a tiny symbol display on a watchband around his wrist. There was room on it only for symbols representing the most basic things the child wanted to say, but these were always with him, and he could point to them right on his wrist.

A child who can move only his foot may have symbols on a cylinder that he moves around until he gets the one he wants. Some children get mixed up when they see a lot of symbols all at once. They may do better by using a disk that can be turned to show only one symbol at a time, like the games in which you turn a wheel to get your answer.

Most of the children have seen the symbols they choose written down by someone else. It is only natural that in time they want to learn how to write themselves. There is a vast difference between putting your own thoughts in written form and depending on someone else to do it for you.

Quite early, the children are encouraged to scribble. This is an important beginning for them even if the lines they draw go wild. Some children must have the pencil or crayon attached to one hand.

When they are older, about the time they are learning to read, a few of the children will develop enough control of their arms and hands so they can write. Most will not. But many can learn to use an electric typewriter that has a special guard to keep them from punching unwanted keys. These typewriters require only a very light touch, but some of the children cannot even manage that. They may still be able to type, by using a head stick with a metal rod to tap the keys. Thus the children can express themselves not only in symbols but also in written words.

Children communicate with Blissymbols first of all at school and at home. This can be satisfying enough for young children who are not yet ready to broaden their horizons. But any intelligent person, child or adult, in time will want to reach out to people in the world beyond his everyday environment. What happens then to these symbol people? Are they understood? Not always. Much depends on the interest and goodwill of the "listener" as well as the training and skill of the symbol user.

Learning this kind of communication is quite different from learning to talk, though both have the same purpose. To make this clearer, perhaps it would help to summarize the stages a child (or adult) goes through in learning symbols. First of all, the child discovers that "symbols do what talking does." Then he is taught symbols and their meaning, slowly, one by one, often with pictures to clarify the meaning. He uses the symbols over and over again once he knows their meaning; they become part of his "speech." Gradually he learns that a symbol may represent a group of related meanings, not just one word. As he comes to understand the logic of the symbols, he discovers that he can combine them and express his thoughts and feelings almost as if he could speak. "Symbols do what talking does."

The teacher will use many devices in teaching the symbols: stories, games, different arrangements of symbols, contacts with other children and adults.

A young child who is learning to talk expects to be understood even if he or she can say only a few words. The beginning symbol user, likewise, expects comprehension on the part of others if he uses any symbols at all. And he *will* be understood, as long as he is communicating with a sensitive instructor, his family, and other people who know him and are aware of his needs and his experience. When he moves beyond this limited circle of people, he cannot expect the same degree of understanding.

He must learn, little by little, to "say" more—enough, in fact, to explain himself to people who know nothing at all about symbols as a means of communication. This of course is difficult. Consider how this differs from learning to speak. A young child hears other people speaking around him and imitates them; this is his principal way of learning. He also imitates the gestures people use. He may nod his head to mean yes and scowl when he is angry or shake his fists at the ceiling. The nonspeaking symbol user, on the other hand, not only has few examples he can imitate outside the instruction room, but he may be unable to make gestures at all, and his facial expression very likely does not correspond with what he wants to say.

There are other difficulties. People do not always respond to his symbols in a way that tells him whether they understand. If, for example, he says in symbols, "I saw a good football game on television yesterday," and the listener says, "Oh," the symbol user is stumped. Did the listener understand what he had tried to say? Was he just uninterested—or baffled? If he could speak, he could solve the problem by asking—but then he wouldn't have needed symbols in the first place. Much more than speaking people, the symbol user must learn to judge the degrees of understanding of the people he communicates with and their willingness to "listen" to his symbols. Then, if he is skillful, he can adapt his symbol-message to the listener. It takes most symbol users years to reach this degree of competence.

At first, using Blissymbols may seem only slightly less frustrating than not being able to communicate at all. The symbol user *is* different from other people, and he knows it. Most speaking people want to help when they come in contact with someone who cannot speak, but often they do not know how. They may do all the wrong things.

Helen's experience illustrates this. Helen has cerebral palsy and spent nine years of her childhood in an institution. By the time she was a teenager she could manage her body fairly well, but her speech was very limited. Only people who knew her well could understand anything she said. Because of this she had been taught Blissymbols, and the 400-symbol board became her constant companion.

Helen then joined a Cooperative Living Project in which she went to live with a young woman named Randy and her husband and another girl who had cerebral palsy. Together they did the household tasks, and the girls went to a special school. Helen was learning to live outside an institution. Randy was discovering the joy and satisfaction of sharing quarters with two lively and attractive teenagers who were finding their way in the world.

Independence was of first importance to Helen, and this meant using her Bliss board wherever she was, both at home and outside. So she used the board at school and took it when she went shopping or to the bank or to a party—wherever she might meet people. Randy went with her; she knew that Helen might have a hard time at first because people would not know how to react.

Sometimes, in fact, people who had never seen a Bliss board would shout at Helen as if she were deaf or talk about her among themselves as if she did not understand. Others would panic because they thought they had to use the board in talking back to her. Sometimes Helen just felt like giving up and going home. But she wanted to reach out to people, and she knew this was the only way she could do it. Randy would explain the board to people, and then most of them were glad to help. As time went on, Helen had many friendly conversations with people she met. Without her Bliss board, this could never have happened, and she considers it worth all the frustrations she has had to go through.

A woman once said to Randy, speaking of Helen, "Poor little thing—she can't talk." At this Randy threw up her hands. "*Can't talk?* She never stops!"

Some symbol users develop so much skill that they can express very complicated thoughts in complete sentences. They can convey their feelings, give commands, ask questions, indicate past, present, and future action, and much more. This is not just a matter of translating spoken words into symbols. Speech is heard; symbols are seen. As we have already observed, this is a significant difference. Symbol sentences may be put together quite differently from spoken words and yet express similar ideas. As time goes on, the instructors and others who work with symbol users will continue to study how this happens and understand more about it. Then the symbol users can be helped to "say" even more.

Blissymbols have done so much for the nonspeaking people who communicate with them. You might think that everyone who has contact with these handicapped children would welcome the symbols with a cheer. But putting across a new idea is seldom easy; this is no exception. Charles Bliss found this out when he launched what he then called Semantography.

There are those who ask, "Won't a child seem too different if he communicates with symbols? People may shy away." This is an understandable question, but experience with symbol users has shown that what happens is just the opposite. Open-minded newcomers are intrigued by the symbols as a way of "talking." They are impressed with the children's ability to relate to others. A child sitting alone in a wheelchair, wordless and isolated, is the one who is too different. Symbols can help make him one with the rest of humanity.

There can be difficulties, too, when people think they must learn the symbols themselves in order to communicate with a symbol user. We have seen how this happened with Helen. The problem vanishes when people see that the related word is printed above each symbol.

The symbol system may seem at first like just another set of gimmicks to the teachers of nonspeaking children. Or the symbols may seem almost too neat and pretty to be practical. Other teachers, seeing this arrangement of lines and circles on a page, decide the system is too complicated. A busy teacher has enough to do without learning a whole new language. And if the symbols look complicated to the teachers, how will the children be able to learn them? Actually, the letters of our alphabet printed on a page look confusing, if not completely mysterious, to a young child who has not yet learned to read. (Look at a book printed in Greek or street signs in Arabic or Russian, and you will get the idea.) Yet children do learn to read. Blissymbols are much easier to learn than our printed words, and they are constantly being simplified as work proceeds.

Very well, the teacher may say, children can learn the symbols. But should they? What is wrong with the way I have been teaching? The answer is that no way of teaching is wrong if it represents the best knowledge available at the time. Blissymbols may be the best means of communication for many children. No one has claimed that they are suitable for *all* nonspeaking people. We will of course know more about this as time goes on.

Fortunately many teachers have gladly accepted symbols as a way of helping nonspeaking children. Such teachers deserve every encouragement they can get, for it is not easy to learn an entirely new way of practicing one's profession. Getting to know the symbols, choosing the right ones for each child, making up special display boards, planning the teaching step by careful step—all this demands many hours of patient work. Teaching the finer points in symbol communication requires knowledge of just what communication means to people and the ways in which our language is used to help people understand each other. These dedicated teachers have made an important contribution to the education of nonspeaking children and adults—how important, we are just beginning to comprehend.

Parents are sometimes hesitant about Blissymbols for their children. They want the children to do normal everyday things, and this means learning words, not those strange symbols. It may be hard for parents to realize, at first, that the child can in time have both—symbols for "talking," printed words for reading.

Most of the parents are enthusiastic about the symbols. You can imagine what it means to a mother or father when a nonspeaking child is able to share his feelings for the first time. Teachers are thrilled to see the look of astonished joy on a parent's face when her child points to the symbol for *mother* on her arrival at school. Some parents do believe their nonspeaking child has intelligence, but the child can never show this to others until he learns Blissymbols. One mother said of her boy, after he had been communicating for some time with symbols: "He is a different boy; now he has a personality."

In the chapter on Kari you will see how much the understanding and encouragement of her mother and father contributed to her success in her struggle with cerebral palsy. There is a similar story in the lives of other handicapped children. One mother wrote this about her child:

> My son John is very severely handicapped by cerebral palsy. Not only is he mute, but he has intense difficulty in controlling his physical movements. As such, it has been very difficult to assess his intelligence. The experts have had difficulty, that is. I have never given up on him since I saw him at four years old, lying on the floor like a broken doll, as I watched him very slowly stick out his foot to trip his brother and roll away with a devilish grin when he was successful.
>
> At home we had always seen a sensitive child with a zany sense of humor beyond his experience and years. Somehow he made his wishes and reactions known by pointing, twenty questions, and just plain E.S.P. His family and our more intimate friends tend to forget his disabilities in their understanding of his personality. . . .
>
> When using his Bliss board, John's movements are laborious, and it takes us a long time to "talk" to each other. Because of the tremendous effort involved, his communiqués are necessarily simple in nature, but what his telegraphic sentences do convey to me is a pathetic awareness of his problems. One day he repeatedly banged at the symbol for *angry* and the message was, "ANGRY, ANGRY, SICK, WANT WALK, TALK" and when he is lonely, I hear "WANT FRIENDS PLAY GAME PLEASE PHONE." . . .
>
> In a very dark room, a very little light shines like a beacon. The shining smile on John's face as he goes off to school each day, the pride with which he sits more upright in his chair and his little stories about school are more than enough miracle for us.

The people who work with Blissymbols do believe in miracles.

·8·

Kari

On the title page of the story of her life Kari wrote, "Handicaps Can Be Hard! This is a True Story. Please Believe the Handicaps."

Kari was thirteen years old when she began to write her autobiography. She had come a long way. Until she was seven, the age at which we met her at the beginning of this book, she had not been able to get across to anyone a single thought or idea. She would try and try; there was so much she wanted to say. But instead of words, out came guttural sounds. Her mother and father did their best to understand, but usually they could not. Kari would finally bang her wheelchair tray, put her head down, and cry with frustration. There seemed to be nothing anyone could do.

"I couldn't talk," Kari wrote, "so my mom and dad had to guess what I was saying. It was so hard for them to guess what I was saying."

Kari had been taken to the Ontario Crippled Children's Centre in Toronto for treatment. The therapists there gave her some exercises and showed her parents how to teach her to chew her food and to sit in a high chair, held up by straps. (Later her father bought her an electric wheelchair.)

The chapter in which Kari tells about her early days at the Ontario Crippled Children's Centre is titled: "I Love You with All My Heart."

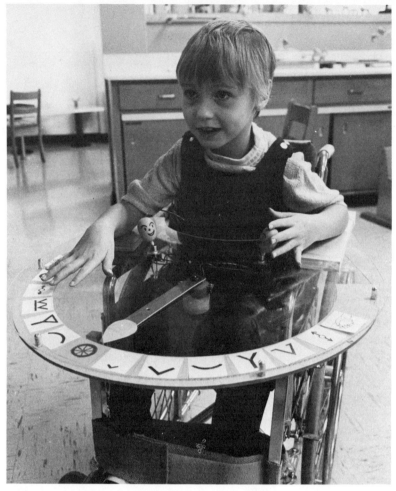

Seven-year-old Kari with her first symbol display.

"My mom was caring for me," she wrote, "and my dad too. I learned to sit up with my legs crossed, but it was hard for me."

No one, however, could teach her to make those incomprehensible sounds into words. The years went by without anyone having much idea of what was going on in Kari's head. Then came symbols.

"When I was seven years old," Kari wrote, "I learned to talk without using my mouth or using sign language. Mrs. McNaughton met the man who was hoping somebody would use his symbols. His name was Mr. Bliss. First I learned a few, then one hundred, two, three, four. It wasn't hard to learn. . . . The first time I took my symbol board home, my whole family was really surprised."

The first symbol board used by the children consisted of about a dozen symbols arranged in a semicircle on a tray fastened above the lap. The child would learn to move a pointer shaped like an arrow to the required symbol. This is the board Kari was using in the appealing picture that was sent to Mr. Bliss in Australia.

Of course twelve symbols were soon too few. Within a few weeks they had to be replaced by thirty, and not long after that, as Kari says, the boards with 100 and more symbols were developed.

Kari's parents were so proud of her. She could come home

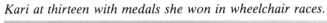

Kari at thirteen with medals she won in wheelchair races.

and tell them what had happened at school and in the taxi that day, and then she would make things up just to keep their attention. Best of all, she could tell them how she felt. It was an important time when she could say, "I angry!"

$$\underset{\text{\rule{0pt}{0pt}}}{\perp_{1}} \quad \times \overset{\vee}{\heartsuit} \langle\!\langle \; .$$

When she wanted to talk, Kari would point to her mouth. Sometimes she pretended she had something to say just because she wanted her mother to come. Before long, symbols decorated the kitchen walls, placed there by Kari's mother so she could communicate with her while she worked.

Kari's mother and father had always loved her and tried to help. But now they began to look at her in a new way. No one had really known how much Kari could do, and certainly no one had expected much of her. Now she could make suggestions and ask questions and get more attention from everyone. She was really one of the family.

In a talk given on television, Kari's mother told some of their experiences: "I thought she was just a lovely, adorable child who could probably not do very much." But she discovered that Kari was much more than that.

Other people changed their attitudes, too. One time a friend of the Harringtons came to visit at the family's summer cottage. She got involved in a lengthy conversation with Kari's mother in which she ignored Kari completely. But Kari was not to be left out. She wanted to question something her mother's friend had said, so she pointed to her mouth, then to her symbols. "How do you know?" she asked. The friend had more respect for Kari after that.

Once Kari asked how a baby gets into the mother's tummy and was told that it grew from a seed. Kari was upset. A few days earlier, while eating an orange, she had swallowed a seed. On her Bliss board, she asked an excited question: "I eat fruit. Baby in me?" It took some explaining on her mother's part to straighten out the confusion.

Kari quickly learned how to combine symbols to get new

meanings and how to use the opposite meaning symbol. Sometimes her combinations were ingenious. One evening at the summer cottage, Mrs. Harrington was so tired she didn't see how she could do anything else at all. She had been taking care of her family, and especially attending to Kari's needs, all day. But Kari did not consider the day finished. "I want to go on boat ride," she said in symbols. Her mother told her to do something on her own instead. Kari was mad. Just saying she was angry wouldn't tell how mad she was. She felt ready to explode, but there wasn't any symbol for *explode* on her board. That didn't stop Kari. She thought fast; then, while her mother watched, she pointed to symbols that meant, "I am going to—like fire!"

I   am going to,   like fire

Her mother was puzzled. She was used to figuring out whatever Kari had to say, but this didn't make sense. "Like fire?" What could that have to do with Kari?

Kari pointed to more symbols:

Like   you   say   to   brother

Kari's mother knew very well what she said to Kari's brother when she was angry. "Oh," she said, "you're about to explode!"

A big hug stopped the explosion.

Not long after this Kari had an operation on her legs, to keep them from crossing one over the other. She had been carefully warned that this operation would not make it possible for her to walk, but she could not stop hoping. One night after Kari came home from the hospital, her mother heard a sad whimpering sound coming from Kari's room. She rushed in and found Kari all crumpled up on the floor. She comforted her daughter and lifted her back into bed, but Kari was still upset. "What's wrong?" her mother asked.

Kari wanted to talk with her symbol board, but she did not want the light on; a flashlight would do. She had dreamed, she said, that she could walk, and so she had gotten up and tried. She had fallen down all in a heap. Later her mother said, "I cried along with her over that one." She was so grateful for Kari's symbols. How could she have known what to say or do if she had had no way of knowing what was bothering Kari?

Kari and her class at Ontario Crippled Children's Centre all took part in the film *Mr. Symbol Man.* Her chapter about that is called "Now I Am a Movie Star." She was not exaggerating; Mr. Bliss thought Kari "stole the show."

"My whole class became a movie star," she wrote. "Bruce Moir made the film. It was all because we used symbols. So it was called *Mr. Symbol Man,* that is Mr. Bliss. . . . Bruce Moir came to my house, and my whole family was a movie star except my sister. She was upset because they cut her out. When my dad and mom were talking, my brother and I were playing house. And Robbie said, 'The children are coming home, what is for lunch?' I said, 'Long food.' " Spaghetti is Kari's favorite food!

For five more years, Kari flourished at the school at the Ontario Crippled Children's Centre. She learned to communicate very well with symbols, and her skill at whizzing around in her electric wheelchair gave her considerable independence. She could have stayed at the center a few more years, but Kari had other ideas. For a long time she had wanted to go to the same school as her brother and sister, near their home in Markham, outside Toronto. She especially longed for this change when her mother woke her at six thirty in the morning to get her ready for the long taxi ride to the center.

Kari wrote: "Mrs. McNaughton thought I was so good at O.C.C.C. school that she talked to my mom . . . about me going to the same school as my sister and my brother. I met my teacher, Mrs. Mann. I visited the school three days in a week. Then I went for all the time."

Mrs. Harrington wrote about Kari's change of schools in the *Newsletter* of the Blissymbolics Communication Institute: "She thought it would be great to drive to school in her new electric wheelchair, go out to play at recess, and to come home for lunch at noon. These things were a 'big deal' to her, and I really don't think she ever thought too much beyond them. Our personal feelings went much deeper than that. . . ."

Fortunately, the Special Education Class for the whole county happened to be at the local school. It was just a five-minute wheelchair drive up the street from the Harrington house. No curbs or barriers blocked the way. The school was built entirely on ground level, with one step at the entrance. Soon after Kari started attending, a ramp was built so she could keep right on going in her wheelchair, over that step and into the school. (There was already a ramp at the front entrance of the Harringtons' house.)

"We were very aware of the feelings Kari might have," her mother wrote, "being the only one confined to a wheelchair in a school where there were hundreds of running, jumping, boisterous children. Already, we had many occasions when she was dejected because of the unfairness of her lot, and, if anything, this new setting could only intensify those feelings. However, her wheelchair and her physical limitations are the facts of life which she must face and accept. Keeping her in a more protected setting wasn't going to change this. Knowing how much spunk she really has, we felt she could cope."

It was reassuring to know that Kari's teacher would be Gwen Mann, a superb teacher who knows a great deal about children with learning disabilities and who has the warmth and understanding these children need so much. Mrs. Mann also believes that, if it is at all possible, it is best for a child to attend school in his or her home community. She welcomed Kari.

Before Kari joined her class, Mrs. Mann learned about symbols at O.C.C.C. and talked with Kari's teachers there. She felt she would be able to understand what Kari was saying. And so she did. As Kari's mother said, "Somehow, she tuned in quickly to Kari's combination of symbols, words, body language and whatever else she happened to use to get a message across.''

The program in Mrs. Mann's class is described in more detail in the last chapter of this book. Except for some group activities, each child has his own course of study, adapted to his special needs. Kari's program was planned as a continuation of her work at the Ontario Crippled Children's Centre; the transition from one school to another was remarkably easy.

Of course there were problems. Kari needed help in going to the toilet. Her mother was willing to be on hand to do this; in fact, she was hired as a half-time teacher's aide for the class. Mrs. Mann thus allowed a mother of one of her children to take part in her class program, something many teachers would find difficult. Kari did not appreciate having her mother there, however. She wanted to be independent. "We made a pact at the start," her mother wrote. "Except for the toileting and help in the gym, she will mind her own business and I will mind mine. I try! Sometimes I overstep the mark, though, and Kari puts me back on line. If the roads are clear, she won't even walk to school with me!"

But the roads were not always clear, and electric wheelchairs are not made for pushing through snow. Some winter days the school seemed to Kari's mother a hundred miles away as she pulled and pushed and hauled a regular wheelchair to get Kari to school. "And all those winter clothes!"

Yuck!

Snow tires for the electric wheelchair helped. Then the Department of Roads cooperated by making the Harringtons' street the best-plowed road around, with generous sanding and salting.

What of the future? "Who knows?" Mrs. Harrington said. "I wouldn't want to turn back for anything, but where Kari's capabilities will lead her remains to be seen. For now, it is a beautiful thing to stand on my driveway and watch her head off to school on her own. More beautiful still is the smile on her face as she turns around to make sure I'm not following her."

Kari has become quite well known, not only because she was one of the first symbol users, but because she was also one of the first to enroll in a regular school. People from all over the world have come to visit her at school.

"When I was in Mrs. Mann's room," Kari wrote, "a boy named Billy Bartlett was learning to talk with symbols. People were interested in the film of *Mr. Symbol Man*. Some people started to visit Billy and me. They didn't come just from Canada. They came from Australia and New Zealand and other countries. Because they were interested in symbols. Some people were teachers and their children can't talk and they are learning to talk with symbols."

"I Really Am a Movie Star Now." That is the title of Chapter 13 of Kari's autobiography. Sure enough, the Canadian Broadcasting Company made a film about people with cerebral palsy, called *The Nature of Things: People You Never See*. The star of the first part of the film was Kari Harrington, just Kari.

She wrote: "In March in Mrs. Mann's room an exciting thing happened. Elizabeth McCallum came with three men . . . to film me. They filmed me typing, working, talking, playing outside and singing in the room that I went to. After school they came to my house to film me getting out of my school chair, Robbie putting Heidi our dog on my lap and Linda and I baking a cake. They filmed some CP people in a town house."

Kari was her usual captivating self in the film, and this time Linda was not left out. The second part showed cerebral-palsied adults living in a residence especially designed for their needs. There, in their wheelchairs, they are able to manage practically everything themselves, in and out of elevators, working at kitchen counters built just the right height—everything. What these people need most of all is to be able to do things for themselves, and the film showed how this is made possible at MacLeod House. Cerebral-palsied people, and those with similar handicaps, have too long been hidden from the rest of us. This is gradually changing. As we see more and more of the disabled, we can begin to understand their need for dignity and independence and learn to accept them as people worth knowing.

Kari spent two years in Mrs. Mann's class. Then, as Kari wrote, "When 1977 came, I went to Mrs. Glanfield's class. Mrs. Glanfield's class is for bigger kids. . . . I learned a lot of things and the doctor said [when she was small] I won't learn much."

The children in her class raised money to buy Kari an electric typewriter, so she could use it in school. (Her parents bought her one to use at home.) In time, however, after months of painstaking practice, Kari learned to write with her left hand, the one she had always used for pointing. She then gave the school typewriter "to my friend Kevin to use at school." Her autobiography is set down entirely in her own careful writing, thirty pages so far, with pictures in color by Kari.

Kari still communicates mainly by pointing to symbols with the forefinger of her left hand. A favorite of hers now is the symbol for monster!

In addition to the set of more than 500 symbols on the board attached to her wheelchair, she has a folding set that is sometimes easier to use in the classroom. On this there are groups of symbols classified according to use—for math, for instance.

"There's practically nothing she can't do," Mrs. Glanfield said. "And she even asks for homework."

It takes a great deal of time and patience and plain hard work to care for a seriously handicapped child at home. Mrs. Harrington has always felt it was worth it.

"People use the word 'burden' to me sometimes," she said when Kari was younger. "But these kids—and I'm not just speaking about my daughter—bring more love with them than a normal child does. Perhaps it's because normal ones have more outside influences and distractions. I don't know. But I see a special sensitivity among cerebral-palsy children. They have a special *something*. And Kari—well, Kari's a real joy."

And now? Kari is growing up. She's "an interesting young lady with a delightful sense of humor."

Kari has come a long way.

·9·

Other Children
Find Their Way

The first "symbol children"—there were originally just ten —had a special feeling for one another. For each of them, the others were the first children they had ever "talked" with. Making contact with other children, not just teachers and parents, helped them to feel they were part of the real world.

Most of the children continued for a number of years to live at home and go to school at the Ontario Crippled Children's Centre. But in time, most left, and the group was scattered. Kari, as we have seen, went to a school in her home neighborhood. Others, still living at home, attended other schools, and still others were sent to special institutions. One of these was John Dowling. John's mother had to work, and the time came when she could no longer care for him at home, so John went to live at Bloorview Children's Hospital in Toronto, where he shared a room with one of the other "symbol children." The hospital is a residence and school specially adapted for the handicapped, rather than a hospital in the usual sense. John can move about freely in his electric wheelchair, from floor to floor in elevators, down corridors, through doors that open for him. He can greet his visitors at the door of Bloorview and take a whirl with them around the gardens.

John was quick at learning symbols from the very beginning. He learned thirty-six in the first two weeks of school at

O.C.C.C., and then three to five every day. He was the "narrator" in Shirley McNaughton's book for children, *Symbol Secrets,* and he has kept his wonderful sense of humor.

At Bloorview John Dowling still communicates with symbols, pointing quickly with his left hand. The letters of the alphabet are printed across the top of his symbol board, so he sometimes spells out words instead of using symbols. John has learned a great deal and done a lot of thinking. You can have a good talk with him, and now and then a good laugh.

John has tried hard to learn to speak, but most people still cannot understand what he is saying. He can talk with his mother without pointing at symbols, but he will probably always need them for communicating with most other people.

Children in many places are learning to reach out to others through symbols. As they grow older, some feel that it is not enough just to use symbols for the business of getting along in the everyday world. They want to be creative, to share with someone their own special feelings about themselves and the people they love.

John Kinnaird wanted to write poetry. He is severely crippled with cerebral palsy and cannot talk. At his school in Pennsylvania John was taught to read and to communicate by pointing at certain words and phrases. This was much more difficult for John than for most of the "symbol children." His cerebral palsy is of the type called *athetoid.* Not only does he lack control of his muscles, but his arms and legs and other parts of his body jerk much of the time. He cannot control his fingers well enough to point with them or to push a switch. Nevertheless, John did learn to communicate. He did it by eye-pointing. Blissymbols had not been adapted for the use of nonspeaking people when John learned to read. So the communication chart he used displayed words or groups of words in squares, at first just twenty-five. The horizontal rows of squares were colored: red, blue, yellow, orange, green. The vertical columns were numbered at the top: one through five. Around this display were arranged squares colored to match the colors of the rows on the display, and the numbers, one

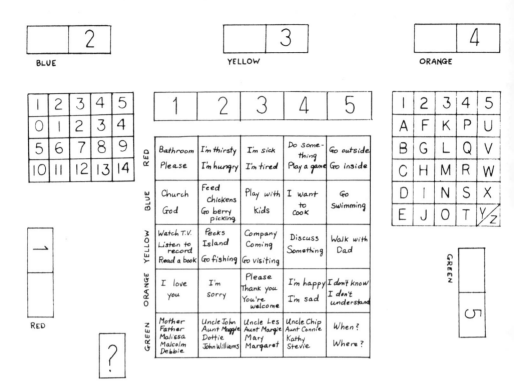

Diagram of an early communication board used by John Kinnaird for eye-pointing.

through five, spaced as far apart as possible. John would choose the word or words he wanted, note the color of the row it was in, and point his eyes toward that color on a square outside the display. That way, whoever was watching would know what horizontal row John's word was in. John would then note the number at the top of the vertical column that contained his word and point his eyes toward that number, outside the display. Colored row and numbered column—that was it, where the two met! Wonder of wonders, John could "talk"—very slowly at first, but faster and faster with practice. He could not have done this accurately by using a standard word board; eye-pointing is not precise enough.

John's poems were written with the ingenious cooperation of himself and two other handicapped people. John would communicate his ideas by eye-pointing to a cerebral-palsied boy who could speak. The boy then spoke the words to still another boy, Paul Klepac, who typed them. This may sound

John Kinnaird and his communication chart.

fairly easy, but Paul, also severely crippled, did his typing with a headstick attached to a helmet. These are determined young people!

When he was sixteen years old, some of John's friends had his poems published in a small paperback volume. The book was called *The Joy of John.* At the front of the book John said: "I'm happy to know my dear friends and family who have help[ed] me and given their time. They were happy to do it. I love them all."

Here are four of John's poems, two from his book and two written since the book was printed:

To Dad

I love you Dad
You don't see the wheelchair
I get on your shoulders
Into the woods we go
You are the best Dad a boy can have.

My Fair Ladies

Five feet or six feet us boys think is pretty
Plump or slim she is a girl
Pretty hair, brown blond or red
All are nice
I love girls

Fathers and Sons

Dad is chasing David while I eat my pie.
I feel their love and imagine
    being a Dad and having a son.
They laugh and play in their love for each other.
I have to think clearly,
So I can be happy listening to them
    instead of being angry at God
    that I won't have a son.

LOOKING OUT THE WINDOW

One big green hill with a boy and girl on it
Laughing and playing in puppy love.
I think of myself and wish and imagine
　in my mind.
　Blue sky, green grass, and a pretty girl and me
　walking on the hill.
But here I am in my chair, looking
　out the window.

The following is part of a section in his book to which John gave the title "Message to My Congregation":

Often I am discouraged, but God is my help when I am sad. I used to be a baby, and then I was a boy. Now, I am a young man and I think like and have the desires of a young man of sixteen.

Sometimes people don't understand this, or if they do understand it, they don't know how to go about including me in their plans.

As John says, he has the same interests and needs as any teenager. Having a crippled body does not change that. He is fortunate in having a family that loves and understands him—even a dad who could take him piggyback on a jaunt in the woods. Life will be easier for many handicapped people when others not only understand their feelings but, as John puts it, learn how to include them in their plans.

Conditions for the handicapped have improved considerably in recent years. In November, 1978, John wrote:

1978

We are so strong and happy.
There's no going back to a day before,
When we were kept hidden in closets.
We look back a few years and see boys and girls
　in their rooms, crying out for help,
　and their parents didn't listen.

But things have changed.
Everyone can go to school since 1973.
By 1976 all the stores have ramps for wheelchairs.
There are newsletters to help us, TV programs
    to help people to understand.

I heard about a lot of people in wheelchairs
    going to Washington.
It makes me so happy to see the progress
    in just a few years.

"Everyone can go to school since 1973"—John was referring
to what has happened since the Rehabilitation Act was passed
by the United States Congress in 1973. This act requires, in
part, that public school districts that benefit from the use of
federal funds (and most of them do) must provide appropriate
elementary and secondary education for all physically or
mentally handicapped children. When this education takes
place in a regular public school classroom, it is called "main-
streaming."

Of course not all nonspeaking people are cerebral palsied.
Some, of all ages, have the equipment for speaking but have
never learned to communicate because they are retarded. A
number of these people can learn to communicate with
symbols when all attempts to teach them to speak clearly have
failed. The connection between their feelings and the symbols
may be simpler and more direct than any connection they can
make with words. They need not understand the theory behind
the symbols, or how the whole system works. If they can use
even one symbol to communicate, that is progress.

Of course they learn very slowly. Some seem able to learn
the meaning of a few symbols but then cannot use them to
communicate anything. Those who can speak fairly well do the
best. There is still much work to be done in determining just
how Blissymbolics can be used with retarded people of any
age. But it seems clear that the symbols can help many of these
people, too, to reach out to the world around them.

Nonspeaking young people who live in different places are

learning to communicate with one another by sending symbol letters. The message is indicated by pointing or by an electronic device and written down by a teacher, a relative, or a friend. This has happened in a school district in Pennsylvania where handicapped teenagers had no contact with anyone their own age until they learned symbols.

Some of these teenagers are mentally retarded. This is David's problem; he is also quite deaf and has never learned to speak intelligibly. In spite of his handicaps, David is quite alert and sociable. He has gotten along well in his special class, especially since he learned symbols. David wrote to Carol, a girl in another school who had already written to him:

$$\text{O} \rightarrow \leftarrow \quad \text{♀C}$$

Hello   Carol

$$\perp_1 \quad \oplus \quad ♡↑ \quad \perp_2 \quad \diagdown \quad \diagdown \quad \boxtimes.$$

I   am   happy   you   wrote   a   letter.

$$\perp_1 \quad ♡+! \quad \boxtimes.$$

I   like   letters.

$$\perp_1 \quad \oplus \quad ♡↑\text{O}.$$

I   am   funny.

$$\perp_1 \quad \pm \quad \text{⚕} \quad \bigcirc_{)(.} \quad \perp_1 \quad \wedge \quad \triangle♡ \quad ·|\ominus.$$

We had snow today.   We   went   home   early.

$$\perp_1 \quad \oplus \quad 16.$$

I   am sixteen.

$$\wedge \quad \perp_2 \quad \pm \quad \hat{\triangle}2 \quad + \quad \hat{\wedge}2. \quad \perp_1 \quad \pm \quad 1$$

Do you have sisters and brothers?   I have one

$$\hat{\triangle}\, 2 \quad + \quad \hat{\wedge}\, 2\,.$$

sister   and   brother.

$$\diagup^{\cdot} \quad \textcircled{1} \quad \overset{\wedge}{\sqsupset}_{1+} \quad \textcircled{\perp} \quad \smile \quad \square\,.$$

This   is   my   head   on paper.

(Picture of David)

$$\overset{\wedge}{\updownarrow} \quad \sqsupset_{1} \quad \sqsupset_{2+} \quad \textcircled{\perp} \quad \smile \quad \square \quad \boxdot \quad \diagdown$$

Give   me   your   head   on paper   in   a

$$\boxtimes, \quad !\heartsuit\,.$$

letter,   please.

$$!\heartsuit \quad \boxed{?} \quad \overset{\wedge}{\sqsupset}_{1+} \quad \boxtimes\,.$$

Please answer   my   letter.

David

This may seem like a simple letter to write. You could sit
down and dash off a letter like that in just a few minutes. But it
was neither simple nor easy for David. He had worked hard
and come a long way before he could write a letter at all. This
one represented his intense yearning to reach out to other
young people—especially to a girl.

Susan Lindsey is a girl in a special class in the same school
district. She is a friend of Carol, to whom David wrote his
letter. Susan's principal handicap is athetoid cerebral palsy,
but she is somewhat retarded as well. Her teacher says Susan is
"quite a lot of fun to know." She has always gotten along well

with her family and friends, but they enjoyed her even more after she learned symbols, and they had a better idea of what she was thinking and feeling.

Susan wrote a letter to a boy named Sam:

Dear Sam,

My friend Carol wrote you [a] letter.

I see T V [at] home.

My friend comes to my home .

How old are you?

Where do you live?

Susan

This letter, as with David's, was quite an accomplishment for Susan and an earnest effort to reach out beyond her lonely world.

Susan also "told" an Easter story to all the children in her school:

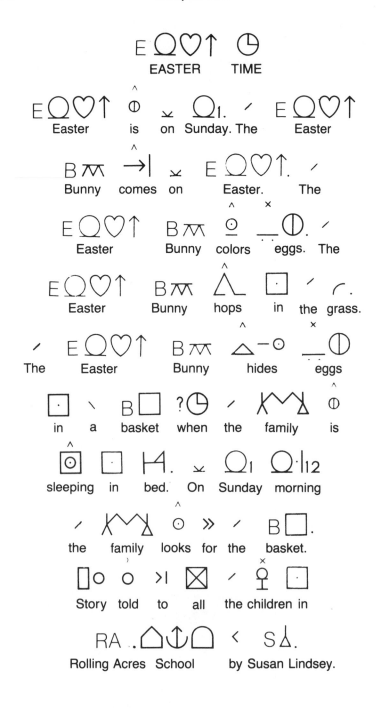

E ⏀♡↑ ◔
EASTER TIME

E⏀♡↑ ⏀ ⏀₁. E⏀♡↑
Easter is on Sunday. The Easter

B⚏ →| E⏀♡↑.
Bunny comes on Easter. The

E⏀♡↑ B⚏ ⊙ _◑.
Easter Bunny colors eggs. The

E⏀♡↑ B⚏ ⋀ ⊡ ⌐.
Easter Bunny hops in the grass.

 E⏀♡↑ B⚏ △⁻⊙ _◑
The Easter Bunny hides eggs

⊡ B☐ ?◔ ⋈△ ⏀
in a basket when the family is

⊙̄ ⊡ ⊢|. ⏀₁ ⏀·|₁₂
sleeping in bed. On Sunday morning

 ⋈△ ⊙ » B☐.
the family looks for the basket.

☐o o >| ⊠ ⚲ ⊡
Story told to all the children in

RA ⌂⏀⌂ ‹ S⟁.
Rolling Acres School by Susan Lindsey.

Never mind that Susan could not literally *tell* her story; the children loved it just the same. Children everywhere are intrigued by Blissymbols. And for Susan, telling an Easter story helped her to feel that she, too, had something to give.

Younger children can send symbol letters, too. Sara, a nine-year-old girl in Florida with cerebral palsy and other problems, until recently had never expected to write letters to anyone.

Robert, another cerebral-palsied child, lives in Ohio. His teacher made a trip to the special school in Florida that Sara attends, to learn about Blissymbols. While she was there, she got acquainted with Sara and asked her if she would like to have a pen pal. Sara would, and thus began a charming exchange of letters between Sara and Robert, which meant a lot to them both.

Here is Sara's first letter to Robert:

November 15, 1978

Hello Robert,

My name is Sara. I have a symbol display. My birthday is after Thanksgiving. I will be nine.

⌐ı ± 3 ⋀,
I   have three animals,

ˋ ⋀ c,   ˋ ⋀ r,   + ˋ ⋀ d, Mimi.
a   cat,   a   rabbit, and a   dog,

?∧   ⌐₂   ♡   ⌐?⌐   ⌐₂   ⊕   ⌐ı₊   ⊥♡+!
How are you? Will you be my   friend?

!♡   ＼   ⌐ı
Please write me.

⌐₂₊   ⊥♡+!   ⚇   S
Your   friend, Sara

Robert wrote Sara a birthday letter and the correspondence flourished. The following February Robert wrote this:

♡›ı   ⚇ S,
Dear Sara,

♡↥   »   ⁄   ⊠.   ⁄   ⊐-♡→
Thanks for the letter — the Valentine.

⚇s,   ⌐₂   ⊕   ⌐ı₊   ″⊥-♡→″.
Sara, you are my   sweetheart.

(This is not the whole letter, but it is the important part.)

Symbol letters are the children's special way of reaching out into the world.

·10·

Adults Talk with Symbols, Too

Blissymbolics are not just for children. Bliss himself devised his symbols as a means of communication for people of all ages. The children at the Ontario Crippled Children's Centre were the first handicapped people to use them because it was their teachers who thought up the idea. But there are more nonspeaking adults than nonspeaking children, and they need help, too. Some of these people have had cerebral palsy all their lives; others are older people who have had a paralyzing stroke that has damaged some of the muscles used in speaking. Many people are also handicapped by not hearing or seeing well, and to some of them symbols are easier to use than printed words.

Often there is no one who can care for handicapped adults at home, and so they must live in special residences or institutions. This need not be a disaster. Institutions can provide facilities that are carefully adapted to the needs of the handicapped. Some are of course better than others.

Gerry Haycock is a young woman in her thirties who is severely crippled with cerebral palsy. She can speak a little, but not clearly, and only those closest to her can understand her. Gerry lives in a cottage with other handicapped women and sympathetic helpers, in a state institution in Connecticut. Often education is not provided for handicapped adults, but Gerry and her companions are fortunate. They are still going to school.

There are many ways of pointing. Gerry uses her toe.

Gerry has been taught to communicate with Blissymbols. The only part of her body that she can move very well is one leg, so she lifts up that leg and points to the symbols on her board with her big toe. When she does not find what she wants on the board, her teacher—or whoever is "talking" with her—will turn the board over. There, on the other side, are the letters of the alphabet, numbers, and colors. Gerry has learned to read, and she can spell some of the words she wants, letter by letter, again pointing with her big toe. Symbols are quicker, but any way is better than nothing when you are reaching out to the world.

When she was twelve years old, after years of speech therapy, Sue Foster was told that she would never be able to speak clearly enough so anyone could understand her, and there was no other way for her to communicate. Sue could hear; she could see. Her quick mind took in these statements; she let them whirl around in her head. Never to communicate with anybody. Never to tell anyone the thoughts and dreams that went on forever within her. Never to say to anyone, "I love you."

Like John Kinnaird, Sue is severely crippled with athetoid cerebral palsy; her arms and legs and head and even her tongue jerk much of the time, and she lives in a wheelchair.

Sue's family love her, but they could take care of her only until she was five years old. From then on Sue has lived in hospitals in Toronto. Until she was twelve, speech therapists had tried to teach Sue to talk, using the best methods they knew, and to read by a phonetic method. Neither worked. Sue could hear spoken words, but she could not speak them herself, and the phonetic approach to reading, relying on the sounds of words, did not make sense to her. She had come to the conclusion that people with her handicap could not learn to read.

But Sue could not accept the idea that she must live forever enclosed in her own loneliness, without any real contact with other human beings. She had a lot to say, to share, and she wanted to do something with her life. There had to be some way for her to reach out. She would watch what other people did. She would try to discover new possibilities in whatever went on around her. There was not much else she could do. She would soon be considered an adult, and there were no funds for the education of handicapped adults.

When she was thirteen, Sue was sent for a few weeks to a summer camp for the handicapped. There she met a nonspeaking girl who had a spelling board and could get basic messages across by pointing to letters one after another. Here at least was one way to communicate. The girl helped Sue learn to spell, one word at a time. By the end of the summer Sue had memorized the spelling of nearly 100 words, and was given her own spelling board.

It was hard for her to point, her hand jerked and wobbled so. But the letters were printed big and quite far apart on her board, and she managed. Now she could at least ask for a drink of water or "say" when she needed to go to the toilet—if someone would look. (And if no one looked, she could make noises to attract their attention.)

But the spelling board, though it brought about a great improvement in Sue's life, was not enough. It was so slow—

and there were so many things she still could not say.

When she was sixteen, Sue was moved from the children's hospital where she had spent most of her life to a residential hospital for handicapped adults. There she met Art Odell, a man who was also crippled with cerebral palsy but who could speak. Art became Sue's constant companion and her voice. Together, each in a wheelchair, they would go about the corridors and recreation rooms at the hospital. Art loved Sue, and he knew better than anyone else what she wanted to say. Sometimes he seemed to know this before she had spelled out a single word. To Sue he was not just a presence and a voice; he was the closest and most loving friend she had ever had. When she was twenty-four years old, she and Art were married.

In the meantime something marvelous had happened. Three years before she married Art Odell, a friend had told Sue about Blissymbolics. Sue made excited noises. Surely this was what she had been hoping for! A symbol board was obtained for her from the Blissymbolics Communication Institute. There they were on the board, 400 symbols accompanied by the English words.

Sue could not read most of the words on her board, of course, but she could point and she could ask. For the next few weeks she asked Art, or she waylaid anyone who was passing by in the hospital and asked the meaning of a particular symbol. Once she knew, she seldom forgot. She was driven to remember; the symbols were her passport to the world of people who could speak.

Within two weeks Sue was using most of the 400 symbols. She was no longer alone, with only Art as her voice. Now she could "speak" for herself, and she could reach out to Art in a new way, telling him in symbols and words of her love and concern. For Art was not well. He was so doubled over with cerebral palsy that it was hard for him to breathe properly, and his internal organs were all crowded together. When Sue and Art had been married only a little more than a year, he contracted pneumonia and died.

Art's death was a devastating blow for Sue. The people who were taking care of her could see that she needed very special

Shirley McNaughton with Sue Odell.

help, so a committee was set up for the express purpose of working out a good program for her. Sue was studied, to see how much she was able to do; then a new wheelchair was provided, better adapted to her needs, and her reading ability was tested. She scored at the early second-grade level, since the only words she knew were those printed on her symbol board. Here was a place where she could really be helped, for Sue was determined to learn to read better than that.

The lack of a paid reading teacher was a problem, but a volunteer might be willing to come once a week. And perhaps in time she could work with other adult students who, like her, were learning for the first time. That would be better than always being tutored alone.

Important as reading was to her, Blissymbols remained Sue's principal way of reaching out to others. With special help from Shirley McNaughton herself, she learned to use all categories of symbols: the parts of speech, indicators, time, tense, almost everything. She could compose long sentences and use opposite meanings and the negative. Sometimes her communications were quite colorful. "I have a bone to pick with you," she began one day.

It was a high point in Sue's life when she and Shirley conducted a church service together, twice, at a church in Port Credit, Ontario, and at another in Toronto. The closing meditation was composed by Sue, in symbols: "I know symbols are good because I am a changed person. The self is not as you see on the outside. The other person has to feel with the heart inside your body."

Sue is intensely grateful to the people who have helped her. She especially appreciates the kindness of the doctor who has taken care of her in recent years, whenever she had to be hospitalized. He has taken the time to read Sue's messages, and when he is very busy, he brings along his sons to help. Sue feels they care—they and the nurses, too.

No matter how hard she tried, Sue's pointing was erratic, and it was often difficult for people who were not familiar with the symbols to get her message. This situation improved greatly when Sue was lent a Blissymbol printer. This is an electronic symbol board with a device that prints symbols, letters, and numerals horizontally, with equivalent words in English, on adding-machine paper. The printer, with its symbol board, was lent to Sue only for a certain number of months. During that time she was to try it out and help educators set up a formal study of its usefulness.

The Blissymbol printer works like this: An electromagnet is embedded in a device called an interface, which is strapped to Sue's left wrist, so it cannot get away from her; it has a handle she can grasp. When she holds this device over various symbols on her board, the electromagnet activates special switches, and these in turn signal the printer to print the designated symbols.

The Blissymbol printer gives Sue a much greater number of symbols than before, more than 800, including numerals and letters of the alphabet. Because there are so many, they must be shown quite small on the display—too small for Sue to locate precisely, with or without an electromagnet. However, the Blissymbol printer has been set up to get around this difficulty. The symbols and letters are all in sets of nine, each set in a square enclosed by heavy black lines. Sue notes with her eyes the position of the symbol she wants in its square (by number, one to nine). Then she finds this number in a special set of numbers on the board—numbers printed big enough so even her uncertain pointing can locate the right one. She moves her interface to the number she wants, and this indicates the position of the wanted symbol in its square. Then all she has to do is indicate which square she wants. She does not have to hit the square exactly with her interface; since the symbol's position is known by its number, anywhere on or near the square will do.

Does this seem terribly complicated? It is. But in no other way could Sue, with her inability to point precisely, have so many symbols at her command. Perhaps at some future time someone will invent a simpler way of doing the same thing, but until then, Sue is grateful for what the Blissymbol printer has done for her. She hopes that someday she can have one to keep, and in fact Sue's friends are already planning ways of raising the money to buy one for her.

Sue learned to use this device very fast. I visited her in her hospital only a few weeks after she had acquired the Blissymbol printer, and she already felt quite at home with the new device. She was especially happy to see Shirley McNaughton, who had brought me. This appeared on the tape:

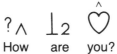

How   are   you?

Asked to produce a combination to mean "author," Sue had the Blissymbol printer print:

person book (to) write

Another visitor asked Sue if she might like to correspond with a cerebral-palsied young man in Florida. Her answer:

① ?

maybe

Then, as we talked about the possibilities of Blissymbolics in
helping nonspeaking children, came this message:

I   like   to learn how young children

can say Blissymbols more quickly now

(than) before. They   are   lucky.

Sue considers herself lucky, too. She knows only too well
how lonely she would be without symbols. Now she has a
purpose in life; by showing what a severely handicapped
person can do, she can help other nonspeaking people,
especially those who have cerebral palsy. This gives Sue
confidence. She sees herself as a "trying" person with "big
feelings," and in spite of the fact that she has never been able
to speak and has spent most of her life in hospitals, she has an
astonishing awareness of the needs and feelings ot other
people.

Sue is learning to read, and later she can learn much else.
One of the first things Sue "said" when she was learning
symbols was this:

I am not mentally handicapped

That's telling them, Sue!

When David Campbell was four years old, he contracted
dystonia, a condition which left him unable to speak or
stand—or even, for many years, to sit in a wheelchair.

David's parents helped him as much as they could; they could see that he was aware of the world around him and interested in what went on. Tutors taught him to read, and he was provided with books, television, and records. In them he found the whole wide landscape of people and ideas. He pondered these ideas; he had his own thoughts about the world, his own feelings about himself and the people who cared for him. Sometimes he did not understand what he read, and he felt frustrated because he could not ask questions. All this was stored up in his mind, year after year.

Then, in the United Cerebral Palsy Adult Center in Ohio, David was taught Blissymbols. In a few weeks he had mastered the 400-symbol chart and devised his own method of indicating symbols. He would point to them with a sort of stick held in his mouth, and he could do this very fast and accurately.

Soon after he learned the 400-symbol chart, David "told" his teacher that he had a question. He wanted a comparison between what the Bible says about the origin of man and what the theory of evolution says about it. Not being an authority on such matters, his teacher took him out to the local branch of the state university to "talk" to a professor in the Department of Religion.

The change in David has been unbelievable. He had been unable to say anything to anybody. Now it became impossible to make him stop. He wanted to get everything out at once, everything he had been storing up for all those years. His parents were fascinated. At last they could communicate with him as they did with their other children, and he had a great deal to say.

Here are some of the things David has said about himself:

"I feel my Bliss board is perfect. It helps me say it all. I can now talk about things I have read [about]—my feelings and my opinions."

"I use my Bliss board to say my prayers—I hope God knows Bliss!"

"I have spent a lot of time in hospitals and would become very upset because I could not talk to my mother about my fears."

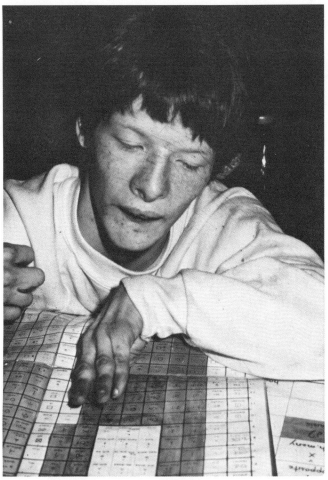

David Campbell with his symbols.

"I like Bliss because I can catch *girls* and talk to them!"

David wanted to go to college. He was bright, he had studied hard, and the local college accepted him. There were many problems; it would take time to solve them all. To get from class to class David would need a motorized wheelchair; this would be very expensive. The Bureau of Vocational Rehabilitation in his city was contacted; would they give David the wheelchair he needed? The answer was no. It seemed unlikely, they said, that David could get a job after he finished college.

Suppose the wheelchair problem were solved, how would David "talk" in class? Reading the words printed on his symbol board as he pointed to them might seem a cumbersome process to people who were unfamiliar with it. A device called Handi-voice might help. David could point to words on this device, just as he does on his Blissymbol board, and the machine would actually speak the words, from a recording. Again the Bureau of Vocational Rehabilitation was contacted; could David have a Handi-voice? Not without going through seemingly endless tests and red tape, and even then he would not be allowed to keep the Handi-voice unless it helped him to get a job. Some other way would have to be found to finance the wheelchair and the Handi-voice.

Even without college, David's life has been transformed because of Blissymbols. No one knows what may lie ahead for him, but it is certainly going to be something quite different from what anyone had ever imagined.

Other people at the Adult Center were learning Blissymbols at the same time as David Campbell. One of these was Charlene Rose. She was twenty-six years old and though she could not speak at all, she had managed to finish the equivalent of three years of high school. Before she was taught Blissymbols, Charlene had used an alphabet board, spelling out words by pointing at the letters. She could also write a little, though with difficulty, and thus could ask simple questions and tell people what she wanted. But all this was much too slow, and Charlene usually preferred to get her ideas across by playing a sort of guessing game with her parents and teachers. This worked up to a point, since the people who were close to her were pretty good at guessing what she wanted to say, but it was very limited. To what extent, after all, can most of us guess what another person has on his mind?

After one day of learning Blissymbols, Charlene pushed away the 100-symbol chart and began on the 400-symbol chart. She was so impatient, she even took shortcuts with that. If she wanted to say, "I like you," she would point to "I—you—like" because the "I" and the "you" are close together. Her teachers had to insist that she could get many more ideas across if she used the chart properly.

Charlene said, "I like the Bliss chart better than an alphabet board because I can speak to someone better. It's too hard to get into a good argument when you have to spell out each word—it just loses something."

And, "It has made me very happy and very excited. . . . It has changed my life because now I can talk to all my friends. My boyfriend can talk to me. I am able to share secrets and deep thoughts with those I care about."

This is what means the most to Charlene—that she can share with others her deepest feelings and the thoughts she had been storing up for so many years.

David Campbell and Charlene Rose have a good deal to look forward to. They were both in their twenties when they learned Blissymbols, and their future looks more promising than they had ever dared hope.

Albert Bancroft, on the other hand, was sixty years old when he encountered Blissymbols. Albert was thought to be somewhat mentally retarded, and he had spent all but eight years of his life in institutions. He was severely crippled with cerebral palsy; as he sat in a wheelchair, his head was bent so far forward it rested on his chest, and his legs were locked together like scissors. Albert could hear well, and he could speak, but the sounds that came out were so strange that it was difficult for anyone to understand him. He had long since learned to expect very little of life. Education had seemed impossible for him, and he had not been taught to read.

Nevertheless, in September of 1976 Albert was sent to the Speech and Hearing Clinic at his institution in Pennsylvania to see if his speech could be improved. When he arrived, he bellowed out to the speech therapist, "Hello, Miss York!" She wondered how he could get the breath to speak in such a contorted position. It was hard for her to understand anything else he said, even though she was trained in understanding difficult speech, but it was clear that Albert wanted help and would do all he could to cooperate. He was scheduled to see the speech therapist every day. Any time would do, Albert managed to say; he never went anywhere.

The therapist decided not to try to improve Albert's speech. It was doubtful that he could change, after sixty years of doing the best he could with his handicap. But maybe Blissymbolics would help. Since Albert could point, it was decided to try. "Yes" and "no" were first taped to the tray on his wheelchair. Then "man" and "woman." (Point: Albert a man, Miss York a woman.) Albert was so bent over that his eyes were just above the tray, which made it hard for him to see or to point, so a new chair was made by the institution's carpenter. Built to accommodate Albert's contorted body, it made it easier for him to see the symbol board. A pointing stick extended his reach. Day after day he learned new symbols by talking and playing games with the therapist. By April Albert could use 103 symbols.

People on the staff of the institution would stop Albert as he went by in his wheelchair, point to symbols, and wait for him to answer. He always tried to speak the word that went with a symbol as he pointed to it. This improved his speech considerably.

Many good things happened to Albert as a result of his learning to communicate with Blissymbols. It was no longer true that he never went anywhere. For the first time in nine years, he was taken on a bus trip outside the grounds of the institution. It was his own idea. Over and over again he pointed to the symbol for *sad* when other patients, not in wheelchairs, went on a trip. Albert's attendants caught on. Soon he, too, was going on trips with other patients in a specially equipped bus.

Albert had been a forgotten patient—his basic needs taken care of, but not much else. Now he had a busy schedule —speech and hearing class, library, bank on Tuesdays, activities class, physical therapy, occupational therapy, and so on.

How could a retarded man of sixty who had been inactive all his life do so much? He probably could not have if he had really been retarded. When she first started working with Albert, Miss York had given him a standard vocabulary test; his mental age scored at three years, eight months. A little over a month after he had begun to learn symbols, he was tested again. His score had gone up to eight years, four months.

About six months later he scored a mental age of eleven years, seven months, and there was no reason to assume he might not go still higher.

Albert had not only learned to communicate but he had discovered himself. The frustration of bottling up his thoughts and feelings was ended. People realized that he had a good mind; they respected him, and he could see that they did. For the first time, Albert was allowed to manage his own financial affairs; he could receive his own checks and bank his own money. This was very important to him.

On his sixty-first birthday Albert was given six birthday cakes by the staff of the institution, by students who worked there, and by volunteers. He shared the cakes with his friends. This, he said, was the best birthday of his whole life.

Still, there was something else Albert wanted above all; he wanted to learn to read. He kept telling this to Miss York. The staff of the institution felt rather uncertain about this, partly because of Albert's age and partly because his learning of Blissymbols had been slowing down. Then the whole idea was postponed because of changes in the staff. For ten months Albert had no language therapy at all. He kept on using his symbols and asking to be taught to read, but anyone could see that he was discouraged.

At last, a program was set up for Albert. He would first be taught to recognize the letters of the alphabet and the numbers one through twenty. This led to a new discovery: Albert could not see very well. This may have been the reason for the slowdown in his learning symbols. Glasses might help; in the meantime Albert's teacher switched to using one-inch letters and numerals, and Albert did very well. Soon he knew the letters and numbers; he began to recognize words. In short, he was learning to read. Progress was slow sometimes; Albert had trouble memorizing anything. After all, he had never had to do this before; his education had been completely neglected. In time, however, people began to communicate with Albert through words instead of symbols. He bought an electric typewriter and had it adapted for his use. That way he could say much more. Meanwhile the number of symbols on his Bliss

Katie, who has cerebral palsy and is very bright, learned to communicate with Blissymbols in her institution in Connecticut.

board had increased to about a hundred. However, he used it less than before, now that he could read words.

More good things kept happening to Albert. A visiting nurse befriended him and began taking him shopping in nearby towns. He still goes on trips. Twice he went to a summer camp run by the Cerebral Palsy Association. Now and then he visits a young friend, a man with cerebral palsy who lives outside of the institution.

This has been the story of four years in the life of Albert Bancroft, beginning when he first learned Blissymbols. He is living a much more normal life than he ever did in all his first sixty years.

Albert Bancroft is not the only older nonspeaking person who has learned Blissymbols. In Canada, and increasingly elsewhere, people who have lived all their lives in institutions, without being able to communicate with anyone, have been taught the symbols. Now they can "talk" to each other and to visitors. Their days are no longer spent in empty silence.

Teaching Blissymbols to adults is not the same as teaching them to children. Children are accustomed to going to school and learning new things, exploring the world around them, ready for new sensations and feelings. If they have difficulties, they see nothing farfetched in getting special help to overcome them.

The adults you have just been reading about were as eager to learn as most children. But many are not so willing. Symbols may seem strange to them, and older people tend to like and trust only what is familiar. Besides, those who can talk a little may not like to admit that their speech is unintelligible —especially stroke victims, who have communicated through spoken words all the previous years of their lives and cannot quite face the fact that this is no longer possible.

Patients in institutions may be unwilling to take on something that makes them look different from the others, such as a Bliss board fastened to the wheelchair. Also, at first the symbols may seem to them like a childish game. These problems are usually solved when patients meet in groups to "talk" with Blissymbols; then they no longer feel different. The attitude of the patient's friends and relatives is important, too. It helps just to say, "Now we can really talk with you."

The people on the staff of the institution, who work with the patients day after day, also play an important part. As in the case of Albert Bancroft, a casual bit of communication in passing can make patients realize that something good has happened in their lives. People no longer just pass them by; instead, they stop to talk because they get a response.

The symbols on the charts that have been used with nonspeaking children may not be the right ones for adults, especially stroke victims who could speak normally for most of their lives and have different interests. Such patients usually already know how to indicate physical needs. What they want is to talk about what goes on in the world and their ideas and feelings about themselves. For this reason they need to learn quite complicated symbols almost at the beginning. Meaningfulness is more important than simplicity.

Interests vary greatly in any adult group. A former banker may not want to talk about the same things as a former teacher or an artist. Each one needs a special symbol chart. Blank grids and symbol stamps are useful in making up such a chart.

People who can read may at first rely on the word that is printed with the symbol rather than the symbol itself. They learn the symbols later. Why, then, shouldn't they just use a word board? This is possible, of course. But it is slower, and, as we have seen, many of the symbols suggest much broader meanings than printed words. It has been shown, in practice, that nonspeaking people can get across a much wider range of meaning with symbols than they can with words.

Of course, Blissymbols are not right for every nonspeaking stroke victim. Some can no longer concentrate very well, or their memory falters, and they are no longer able to learn a sophisticated new system of communication. The speech therapist is usually the one to decide which patients might benefit from symbols.

David Campbell and the other young people in his adult center had naturally had very limited experience—as little, in some cases, as schoolchildren. Yet they did not want to be treated like children. They were adults, and their interests were much the same as those of people their own age anywhere.

They had listened to rock music on records and radio; now, with Blissymbols, they could talk about it. They had heard other people cracking jokes; now they could make their own. They could show off their skill in using symbols. The young men liked to talk about girls, and the girls liked to talk about men. For them, as for Kari and John Kinnaird, "symbols do what talking does."

·11·

Other Ways

The success of Blissymbolics has been phenomenal, but there are other ways to help people who cannot speak. Ask Ricky Hoyt of Westfield, Massachusetts. He has cerebral palsy and cannot talk, but he will answer you through his computer.

This device is only a little bigger than a bread box. Ricky sits in his wheelchair facing the computer, so he can see it clearly. A panel on the computer displays letters, numbers, and a few simple words and signs, most of them in separate squares. When the computer is turned on, a beam of light jumps from square to square, across one row after another, taking three seconds for each jump. To choose a letter (or whatever), Ricky waits until the beam jumps to the one he wants, then hits a lever on his chair with his knee. The beam stops right there. The letters appear, in word order, on a television screen beside the computer panel; at the same time, the words are printed on paper at the rear of the machine.

Ricky got his computer in 1972, when he was ten years old. He had already learned the alphabet by feeling cut-out sandpaper letters at the same time someone said their names out loud. With cutouts he could spell his name and a few simple words, so he was ready to move on to the computer.

Ricky is an avid hockey fan, and the first thing he said on the computer was "Go Bruins!"

Of course, spelling out words this way, letter by letter, is slower than indicating whole words or ideas by Blissymbols, and Ricky's bright mind works much faster than his machine. Sometimes he gets pretty frustrated. When it's just too much,

he can "swear" by stopping the beam of light at S ✡ ? ÷

This computer is called the TIC—Tufts Interactive Communicator—or the Hope Machine. It was developed by graduate student Rick Foulds and his associates at Tufts University in Massachusetts. Fifteen or more children in Massachusetts are now using TIC's. Ricky used his knee to stop the beam of light because that is where he has the best control of his muscles, but as with Blissymbols, other children use different parts of their bodies. The computer setup is

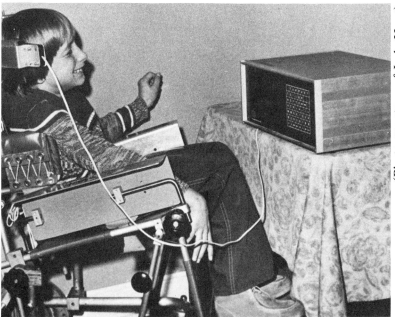

(Photo courtesy of Judy Hoyt)

Ricky Hoyt and his TIC, which he operates with a head switch.

constantly being improved to meet the children's needs in the best way possible.

With the help of a full-time teacher's aide, Ricky began attending a regular public school; a computer there was adapted for his use. From the very beginning, both teachers and children accepted him as a real member of the class. His classmates helped out by feeding him his lunch.

Ricky is now a student at Westfield High School, completely "mainstreamed." Several things have changed: he can now use a head switch as well as his knee, and he is learning to program his own computer.

None of this has been easy. It has required an incredible amount of work and hope on the part of Ricky's family and other people. To raise money to pay for the first computer, the Hoyts put on bake sales, a dinner, and a raffle. But once Ricky got his computer, he could use his intelligence like a normal human being.

The TIC is not the only computer that has been adapted for the use of nonspeaking people. It now has a more sophisticated relative, called TACTIC.

In California, still another computer helps a cerebral-palsied young woman named Rebecca to communicate. Rebecca can read, and before she obtained her computer she managed to make her wants known by using a homemade word wheel. This consisted of a bicycle wheel with a spoke that pointed to letters of the alphabet printed on a round sheet of cardboard. As the wheel turned, the spoke pointed to each letter in turn. Power to operate this ingenious device was supplied by an electric-clock motor, and Rebecca could turn on the power by pressing her knee against a switch (much as Ricky does). When the spoke was near the chosen letter, she moved her knee away from the switch, and this stopped the motor. By this method Rebecca could spell out words at the rate of about one *letter* per minute—better than nothing, but agonizingly slow.

The computer Rebecca uses now was developed by Tim Scully, who is associated with the Langley Porter Neuropsychiatric Institute in San Francisco. Unlike Ricky's computer, this

one displays whole words on a television screen—a vocabulary
of about 1,200 of them, fed into the computer when the system
was set up. These words were first stored in the computer in
alphabetical order, as in a dictionary, but the problem then
was, how could Rebecca choose the word she wanted fast

A New TIC.

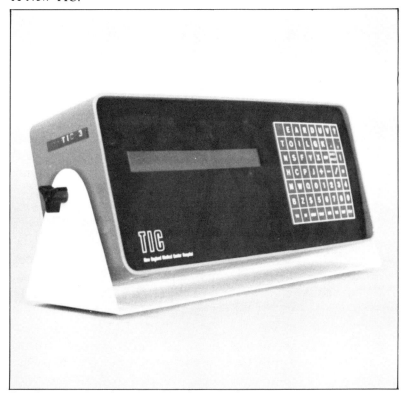

enough? To accomplish this, the words were rearranged alphabetically in groups of 120 each, and these in turn were divided into subgroups of about ten words. Each group has a name that consists of its own first and last words. The groups are first shown by name, one after another, on a special section of the television screen, and Rebecca picks the group that contains the word she wants. (She does this by pressing her knee switch and then releasing it.) The same is done with the subgroups, as their names are offered. Finally, she chooses the individual word she wants in the same way, and it appears on the message section of the television screen. Thus the message is built up on the screen, word by word, to a possible total of 200 words at a time. (The computer automatically leaves a space between words.)

Does this sound too complicated? With a little practice, Rebecca found it remarkably easy, and she can build up a message on that screen much faster than you might think. Her method of choosing words is something like the method Sue Odell uses in choosing symbols, though the purpose is different. In Sue's case the symbols were arranged in groups to help overcome her inability to point precisely. For Rebecca the purpose was to speed up her choosing of words.

Letters of the alphabet are available to Rebecca, arranged in the order of most likely use. She uses these to spell out words that are not included in the computer's supply of 1,200. (Only capital letters are used.) Rebecca can start a new line of words, backspace, add punctuation marks, erase a word or the whole television screen. The system is mounted on her wheelchair.

Rebecca's computer, like Ricky's, is a commercially available one that anyone can buy—at a price. Actually, it is much less expensive than most computers. (Rebecca's cost about $1,300 at the time it was set up.) Blissymbol charts, how ever they are set up, are, of course, cheap by comparison, and that is one reason why they will be available to more people for some time to come. And of course Blissymbols have the added advantage of being practical for young children and others who cannot read. As we have seen, computers that work with symbols are still another possibility.

Rebecca's computer has one very significant advantage over the TIC: it displays whole words instead of letters, and thus is faster to use. On the other hand, Ricky's TIC prints his words, and Rebecca's does not. Tim Scully has since improved his computer to include this feature. Besides that, a message can be changed by "editing"—inserting more words into a sentence or deleting some others and closing up the spaces. The computer user can also now change the speed at which words or letters are presented, to suit his particular needs. In some cases a user can choose whole phrases instead of separate words: "I'm hungry." "Please help me!" "Thank you."

And so on. Tim Scully intends to continue producing better and better computer aids for the handicapped. He thinks that in time devices can be developed that will be so sensitive that a switch could be activated by the twitch of an eyelid. What a boon this could be to symbol users who now struggle with eye-pointing. The possibilities boggle the mind.

Computers have been used, too, in teaching apes to communicate with people and with each other. This is quite different from teaching human children, who, whether they can speak themselves or not, have heard words spoken all their lives and know what they mean. Apes have no understanding of language at all. It is interesting, nevertheless, to see how abstract symbols have made possible a kind of simple communication for them. Moreover, this work has made an important contribution to the lives of some retarded children.

For a long time psychologists have wanted to know whether apes could be taught to communicate by using some sort of sign language. Experiments along this line might teach us a good deal about the development of the human brain from a simpler form to a complex instrument of thought and feeling. For more than ten years extensive work has been done with both chimpanzees and gorillas, and the results have been astonishing. Apes cannot talk; they do not have the necessary physical equipment for producing the proper sounds. But they can use their hands for making signs, and consequently most of the apes that have learned to communicate have been taught the sign language of the deaf, American Sign. Koko the gorilla, for instance, can make several hundred signs with her hands, and she even combines them to make new meanings—such as "finger bracelet" for "ring." Koko also listens to what people say and responds with her fingers.

Sarah is a chimpanzee who has been taught to communicate with abstract symbols. Her trainers supply her with pieces of plastic of varied shapes and colors, and Sarah moves these about on a metal board.

Most interesting for us is Lana, a chimpanzee who communicates in "Yerkish," a system of more than a hundred abstract graphic symbols that she produces by pushing keys on a relatively small computer. Yerkish gets its name from the Yerkes Primate Research Center at Emory University in Atlanta, Georgia, where Lana has been trained by Duane Rumbaugh and his associates.

Lana has a vertical keyboard with one hundred keys. When she presses a key, this sends a signal to the computer, and a "Yerkish word" appears on a lighted screen above the keyboard. At the same time, the computer prints the word in English on punched paper tape.

What does this Yerkish language consist of? As with Blissymbolics, the symbols are purely visual and cannot be spoken. But these symbols, called lexigrams, are entirely abstract forms, not suggesting any concrete object or association of ideas (as a heart shape suggests affection). Each one is made up of design elements that have been carefully constructed, so that they can be superimposed without canceling each other out.

When Lana presses a key, indicating her choice of a certain lexigram, the computer combines two or more of these nine design elements to make the lexigram. Each such lexigram is a Yerkish word, and these are what Lana sees on her keyboard and on the screen above it. Background colors are also used, a different color for each class of words. *Red* for food, for instance, *green* for parts of the body, *blue* for activities.

Here are some examples of lexigrams, showing which design elements each one is made up of, and the background colors:

DESIGN ELEMENTS

1	2	3	4	5

6	7	8	9

Elements 2, 4, 7 Orange	Elements 1, 7, 8 Orange
BLANKET	BOX
Elements 1, 5, 6 Red	Elements 5, 9 Red
NUT	WATER
Elements 1, 3, 8, 9 Blue	Elements 1, 2, 3, 5 Blue
TO BITE	TO GROOM

Lana's design elements and some of the lexigrams that can be made up from them.

Besides these lexigrams there are symbols for *yes, no* (or *not*), *please, question,* and *period.* (Lana ends a sentence properly with a period.)

Lana's training began when she was a little over two years old. From the first she was very cooperative. One at a time she was taught the meaning of the lexigrams, by trial and error or by being shown. At first it was found that she would choose lexigrams by their location on the board, rather than by their appearance. The lexigrams were then moved to new positions, so that Lana would learn to distinguish one from another. Only gradually, however, did a lexigram come to mean food or drink or a happening.

Lana's reward for pressing the right keys was small amounts of food. She could "say": "Please machine give banana," or "Please machine give juice" and the vending machine would automatically comply, producing the banana or the juice in a container just below the keyboard. In the same way Lana could also get music played on tape. All this she could do even when no technician was there. Day and night she had access to the computer. Alone in the middle of the night, she might get up and signal the machine to play her favorite tape. She could also, at any time, ask for movies, slides, or a view of the outdoors.

Lana thrived on social contact, however, and often a technician was with her. The technician had a separate keyboard with which he or she could "talk" to her. Lana learned a surprising number of things on her own, without being taught. She could say "No chow in machine" when there was none. She could combine lexigrams to make new meanings and start a conversation herself.

Here is a sample conversation between Lana and Tim. (The question mark always comes at the beginning of the sentence in Yerkish.)

Tim: ?Lana want apple.
Lana: Yes. (Thereupon Tim went to the kitchen and got one.)
   You give this to Lana.
Tim: ?Give what to Lana.
Lana: You give this-which-is-red.

Tim: ?This. (Tim held up a piece of red plastic as he responded.)
Lana: ?You give this apple to Lana.
Tim: Yes. (And he gave her the apple.)

Conversations with Lana were often tests, to see what she could do. In this case, Tim tried to fool Lana with a piece of red plastic. But that wouldn't do; what Lana wanted was a red *apple.*

Lana learned to combine symbols in somewhat the same way as children do with Blissymbolics. One day Tim appeared with an orange. Lana liked oranges but had as yet no lexigram for one. So, she chose a lexigram for apple plus one for the color orange and thus made her own combination: "Please, Tim, give apple-that-is-orange."

The work with Lana shows that chimpanzees, with the help of people, can learn to use a limited visual language for communication. (No one knows, of course, whether Lana really "understands" the meaning of the Yerkish symbols.) As with any symbols, communication between Lana and her technicians depends on agreement as to meaning, at least in a superficial sense. Perhaps chimpanzees in the wild might have developed a rudimentary sort of language if they could have agreed on the meaning of certain sounds or gestures. But it is thought that they lack the intelligence to do this.

Timothy Gill has worked more closely with Lana than anyone else. Sometimes he wonders just what goes on. When one of his own young children was beginning to talk, he found that she learned much the same way Lana did, though faster.

Then the Yerkes people began to wonder if Lana might be unusually bright for a chimpanzee. After all, her accomplishments only proved what *she* could do, and it was important to find out if other chimpanzees could do the same. In 1976 four more animals joined the project: Sherman, Austin, Ericka, and Kenton. They did not move in with Lana but were taught lexigrams sometimes separately, sometimes together. One animal could learn by observing the other at the keyboard. They mastered Yerkish just as well as Lana, and besides being able to communicate with a human, they could carry on a sort of conversation with each other, in a symbol vocabulary that increased to over fifty words.

Here is a typical episode between two of them: Sherman sees a researcher drop food into a box within his reach. He wants the food, but he can't get it because the box is fastened with a padlock, and Austin has the key. No problem. Sherman goes to his keyboard along the wall and presses the keys that will make the computer produce the lighted lexigrams that mean "give key." Austin, who has been watching all this time, knows what those symbols mean. All right, he'll get the key. He finds it in a tray of tools and hands it to Sherman, who then inserts it in the padlock and unlocks it. Austin watches eagerly as Sherman removes the padlock, opens the box, and takes out the food. He gives some to Austin.

The researchers have a curious feeling that comes to them now and then. It is an astonished realization that somehow, in a totally new way, they have begun to communicate, even to discuss a thing or two, with a chimpanzee.

This is not the whole story, for at some point it occurred to the research people that communication with Yerkish symbols might be helpful to nonspeaking children who are mentally retarded or otherwise brain-damaged. A project was set up at the Georgia Retardation Center in Atlanta, by which a group of profoundly retarded children were introduced to Yerkish. They used the same conversation board as Lana and the other chimpanzees and a similar computer.

Yerkish has brought about a tremendous change in the life of Chris, a girl in her late teens who has a mental age of two and a half years. Chris, though born with the physical equipment for speaking, had never been able to communicate at all. She could not even ask for a drink of water. There seemed to be little meaning in her life, and feeling this in her own hazy way, she had turned into a miserable whining overgrown child. All this has changed. Chris gets up in the morning with a cheerful smile, looking forward to what the day may bring. In the small computer room at the center she punches keys to carry on a conversation with her teacher, Royce White: "Royce give cookie?" She gets her cookie and a hug. Now Chris can live like a human being. When Royce says, "Good job, Chris!" her face shines with joy. She can even *say* some words.

For the first time, Chris has some realization of other people's feelings. When a photographer was having a hard time getting a good shot of the computer, Chris patted her on the shoulder and murmured, "Good job, good job."

Other children and young people at the Retardation Center have learned Yerkish symbols, and some who have tried to learn have failed. Still, it is cause for rejoicing when even a few retarded people can be helped to lead richer lives.

Even severely retarded human beings have a greater capacity for knowledge than chimpanzees. The search will go on for ways to help at least some of these people.

There are limitations in the Yerkish program. Computers are very expensive, of course, and the standard keyboard cannot be carried around. Perhaps portable battery-powered keyboards can be developed. Chris has a nonelectric board she carries around so she can communicate with staff people at the center.

Why not Blissymbolics for some of these children? We have seen how they have been used to help the retarded, and teachers at the Georgia Retardation Center have thought of this, too. In a parallel project, with a different group of children, they are exploring the use of Blissymbolics. As elsewhere, retarded children who had never communicated with anyone are beginning to reach out to their teachers, getting at least a few messages across by pointing to these symbols. Learning Blissymbols is a long, slow process for them, and they cannot yet communicate with one another. Perhaps this will come in time. Blissymbols may well prove more useful than Yerkish because they are so often related to real things, and their simplicity and logic makes them easy to grasp. It is too soon to say how much this will mean to the retarded, but there is hope now where little existed before.

·12·

The Future Looks Bright

Blissymbols have been in active use for only a few years; nonspeaking handicapped people have benefited most. No one knows what exciting possibilities may develop in the future. Already some teachers have started using the symbols with aphasic children. These are children who, though they may be normal in other ways, cannot use or understand language because of brain damage. Billy is one such child. He was in the Special Education Class at James Robinson Public School in Markham, Ontario, when Kari Harrington joined the group. The teacher, Gwen Mann, thought Blissymbols might help Billy, and since he had taken to Kari right away, she began teaching him symbols for a short time every day. Before long he could communicate in sentences made up of symbols, and he had learned to read some regular words.

Mrs. Mann had known about Blissymbols for some time before Kari joined her class, but she had thought they were too abstract for her children. Kari changed her mind about that.

The class numbered twelve children, all of them with learning problems—some aphasic, some with other problems in using language, some with emotional problems, others slow learners. When Kari joined them, everyone became interested in "talking" with her and learning her symbols. Mrs. Mann discovered how easy the symbols are to learn and how naturally they seemed to fit into her language program.

Though at first Billy was the only one really being taught the symbols, all the children were fascinated by them. And two other boys began to get much more interested in reading when Kari pointed to *words*.

One class project was a weather calendar, made by the children and the teacher together. Blissymbols were perfect for that—symbols for sun, rain, snow, wind, ice, and so on, each one looking like a simplified picture of what it was meant to be, and scientifically accurate as well.

As Billy learned more symbols, he could be taught the skills he would need in order to learn to read. Best of all, he could now tell other people how he felt about things. Kari was thrilled with his progress and with her own part in helping him. By the time Kari left the class, Mrs. Mann had decided to use symbols in teaching all the children. Symbols, she had found, could even help some children to understand better whatever was said to them. This was because they could *see* a symbolic representation of things and ideas while they were hearing the words.

In learning to read, any child has to stop from time to time to figure out a word. For these children the process was even slower. Symbols were much faster and easier for them to learn, and as a result, they could feel that here, at last, was something they could *really* do. The pressure to succeed was off; they could relax and be themselves. They loved it. One father was heard to remark at a parents' meeting that there had not been one morning when his little boy was not eager to go to school—something that had never happened before.

Today a visit to Mrs. Mann's classroom reveals Blissymbols everywhere. The children who communicate with them have their own folding charts, made from the new symbol stamps especially for them. The charts are color coded, yellow for things, green for action words, blue for adjectives, and so on. Sometimes sentences are included:

⊥₁ −! ⌒.   ?∧ ⊥₂ ♡
I   don't know.   How are you?
                     (How you feel?)

Each child also has his own book with *his* words and symbols. Lists of words and symbols in various categories are posted on the wall: school, home, weather, months, seasons, and so on. And there is a big general symbol display against one wall, for everyone to see. The progress is from symbols to words.

We should have workbooks for these children, Mrs. Mann thought, and so she and her husband Andy made a whole series of workbooks, based on her work with symbols in the classroom. Symbols and words are combined with interesting things to do. There is a space for the children's own pictures and words about their families, their friends, their pets. These workbooks use most of the symbols in the 400-symbol chart. They are intended to stimulate children to read by themselves, especially those who have had trouble learning to read at all. Symbols on each page help children to understand and remember the words; often they may learn the symbol first and then associate the word with it. At the end of each book is a sort of minidictionary of all the words and symbols used. This can be helpful for spelling when the children begin to write their own stories.

Some children find reading difficult, if not impossible, because they see the letters reversed or because in some other way they do not see words as they are printed on the page. Others are slow in learning to read because of various handicaps. Some, though not retarded, are not very bright and can only learn slowly. For all these children the symbols may provide a transition between familiar objects and pictures and the abstraction of printed words.

A few teachers are beginning to use symbols with autistic children—those who, for reasons that are not understood, are so withdrawn that they do not make contact with anyone. When such a child begins to focus on something, even if it is only a shoelace, and this focusing is reinforced by repetition, this can become a first step towards communication. Focusing on a symbol can then lead to communication with the person who provides the symbol.

Children who cannot hear have very special problems, but they, too, can be helped by symbols. For many years the deaf have communicated by means of signs formed by the fingers and hands, but this sign language requires rather precise control of the fingers—control that very young deaf children may not yet have developed. Blissymbols may be helpful to them and to deaf people of any age who need to communicate with people who do not know sign language.

Terry was a profoundly deaf child in Australia who could not seem to learn sign language and was a disruptive influence in his class. Blissymbols were an immediate success with him. He was intrigued by what looked to him like small drawings of things he was familiar with—house, car, television, eye, nose. After working with a special teacher for just a few days, he had learned 100 symbols, and before long he was tackling the 400-symbol chart. Along with the symbols the teacher introduced the deaf signs, and this time Terry managed them very well. From then on he used both the deaf signs and Blissymbols and began to take part in activities with his class. For the first time, he understood what was going on.

Some children with cerebral palsy are also deaf. Blissymbols may help these the most. One little girl in a school in Middlesex, England, both deaf and afflicted with cerebral palsy, has learned to "talk" with Blissymbols. She loves her Bliss chart so much that she takes it to bed at night.

Alice is a young adult in Scotland with similar afflictions. For the first fifteen years of her life, Alice hardly communicated with anyone. The teachers in her day-care center had tried to help her to talk (difficult with anyone who is deaf) and had attempted to teach her lip reading and sign language. But Alice's head shook so she could not watch a person's face closely, and her hands could not form the signs.

Over the years Alice improved physically, however. By age fifteen she could control her head fairly well and could use her fingers to point. Only her hearing failed to improve. A word board was tried but was not a success, since most of the words still had no meaning for her.

Then a new speech therapist, Clare Latham, was assigned to Alice. She knew Blissymbols and decided to try them. After all, she reasoned, the symbols are visual, and do not depend on hearing. To the therapist's amazement, Alice learned eight pictorial symbols in her first lesson. They resembled things she had been looking at all her life: man, woman, animal, and so on.

The less pictorial and abstract symbols were a different problem—how to teach these visually with no reference to sounds? It is interesting to see how Mrs. Latham contrived to teach Alice the symbol for "I" or "me": $\perp$।
She stood the girl against the wall in front of a long mirror, then she drew two lines on the wall—a long vertical one alongside her and a shorter horizontal line along the bottom where her feet were. Alice could look in the mirror and see herself and the symbol together: Alice . . . me . . . the most important person in my world . . . number one. After that Alice recognized this symbol whenever she saw it. Other symbols, beginning with those for parts of the body, were taught in a similar way—by *showing* Alice their meaning. Gradually she learned not only to recognize symbols but to use them herself.

The question symbol   presented a special problem. Not only is this an abstract symbol, but Alice had had no experience with questions, beyond moving her head yes or no to the simplest queries. Mrs. Latham first showed her some comics in which characters had bubbles coming from their mouths, enclosing short speeches with a question mark at the end. Alice seemed to get the idea. Mrs. Latham then drew herself with a simple question in Blissymbols coming from her mouth:

$$\boxed{?}\quad \perp_2 \quad \heartsuit\!\!+\,! \quad \underset{\_}{\text{O}}$$

Do   you   like   food?

(In Bliss, you remember, the question symbol comes first.)

Alice responded to that by pointing to the symbol for "yes," and Mrs. Latham went on to other questions. Thus, Alice knew how to *answer* questions. But *asking* them was an entirely new concept. For a long time she simply could not seem to do it. Then she was introduced to Ali, a boy her own age who was a nonspeaking symbol user but not deaf. Ali had plenty of questions to ask her; and she answered with symbols. And then, three weeks later, she had a question for *him*:

⌊?⌋   ⌊₂   ♡+!   ⦂

Do   you   like   girl (Alice)?

I like you, "said" Ali, and that was the beginning of a friendship. Alice was no longer alone in her silent world.

Symbols work two ways for the deaf: deaf people can express their own ideas and feelings, and they can receive messages from others. The second of these is at least as important as the first, especially for young children and others who cannot read.

Jimbo found this out. He is an eight-year-old boy who goes to the same school Sara attends in Florida. Technically Jimbo is not deaf; he does hear, but because of brain damage his mind cannot make sense out of the sounds that come to him. This of course has made it impossible for him to learn to speak intelligibly.

Symbols have opened up the world to Jimbo, who takes his Bliss board everywhere he goes. One time his father was going away on business by plane, and Jimbo went with his mother to help see him off. But he was unhappy—he wanted his father to stay home—and he began to "talk" to his parents about this. A flight attendant in the airport lobby saw what was going on. Realizing that Jimbo was upset, he came over and, after watching a while, started a conversation in symbols with Jimbo himself: "Daddy go on airplane, you like airplane?" Still pointing at symbols, the attendant explained his job to Jimbo and told him where he could go to watch him. The boy was fascinated, and he became much too busy to worry about his daddy's leaving. He had a new friend, the flight attendant, and he was going to watch him board the plane. Symbols can work two ways, to communicate a message or to receive one. This time it was Jimbo's *reading* a message that saved the day.

Can symbols help a person who cannot speak and is also blind? As I have emphasized all along, these are visual symbols. Nevertheless, Anthony J. Dipiano, a speech pathologist at the West Seneca Development Center in New York State, thought there must be some way these symbols could work for the blind nonspeaking residents of the Center. Most of the residents were retarded as well, and this did not help. But blind people have a highly developed sense of touch, and this gave Mr. Dipiano an idea. He made a special symbol board for the blind by sticking raised rubber symbols, produced by a company that makes rubber stamps, onto a piece of masonite. This first board was made specifically for George Brown, a retarded resident of the Center who is also blind, hearing impaired, and nonspeaking. He was in his twenties and had never been able to communicate with anyone. George could feel the shape of the symbols with his fingers, just as blind people who can read feel the dots of braille.

This raised Blissymbol communication board is very durable and can easily be carried around. Any symbol can be pulled off the board and moved to another position or exchanged for a different one. They stick! Such a board may even prove useful to other handicapped people—for instance, cerebral palsy victims whose fingers tend to slide off the usual flat board because they cannot control their muscles. Still more possibilities for the future!

Most of the nonspeaking children eventually learn to read. As with any group of children, some can learn more easily than others, and a few may never be able to read. Very little is known, so far, about *how* these children learn, although it is clear that they cannot do so in the same way as speaking children.

Normal children master spoken language long before they enter school. When they learn to read, they associate the printed words with spoken words they have been hearing and saying all along. (Besides this, they can probably recognize some printed words by their shape and general appearance.) They learn that certain letters and combinations of letters represent certain sounds, and when they see these letters, they can say the appropriate sounds. This is the phonetic system of learning to read, and it generally works very well. But nonspeaking children are completely cut off from this method (we have seen how unsuccessful it was with Sue Odell), and this is a serious handicap in learning to read.

A number of techniques are used in teaching reading to nonspeaking people, but they are beyond the scope of this book. For those who cannot learn to read, however, an extension of the symbol system might be developed, with a wider range of vocabulary and new ways of gathering information through symbols.

For those who *can* learn to read, Blissymbols can be a real help. For one thing, the symbols make it possible for nonspeaking children to communicate long before reading is possible for them. That way their minds, instead of going through a long period of stagnation and frustration, can be kept active. Even in their limited world, experiences can be varied and stimulating, promoting what educators call reading readiness. Children who have had a good experience with the people and things around them are ready, at the appropriate age, to learn reading and whatever else they may be capable of. Nothing is more important for learning of any kind, and it is almost impossible without communication.

The logic and clarity of the Blissymbol system helps the children to think clearly. Slower children learn fewer symbols than the bright ones, but all is perceived in an orderly fashion. Such things as the tenses of verbs—past, present, future—are learned much more easily in symbols. For example, how much simpler than the words are the symbols for *go, will go, gone* or *went*:

And how much easier it is to learn symbols when just one symbol can have several meanings. For example:

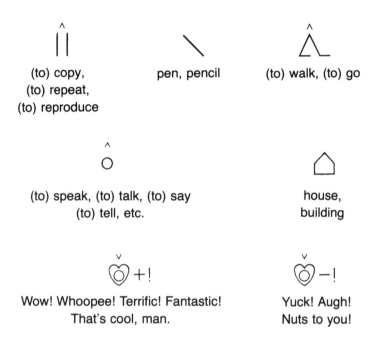

| (to) copy, (to) repeat, (to) reproduce | pen, pencil | (to) walk, (to) go |

(to) speak, (to) talk, (to) say (to) tell, etc.

house, building

Wow! Whoopee! Terrific! Fantastic! That's cool, man.

Yuck! Augh! Nuts to you!

So much can be done with symbols. Finding the right one, thinking up combinations, making jokes—all this stimulates the children's imaginations. It's fun—and sometimes funny. The symbol for *toilet*, for example, is *chair* over *water*. Exactly so.

In the process of using symbols, children see the word printed above each one. Time after time they go over the same symbols and words, until they often recognize the words as well as the symbol. Thus children who cannot speak may get ready to read.

Symbols will never be a substitute for reading, and as we have seen, it was not the intention of either Charles Bliss or the teachers of nonspeaking children that it should be. But they can certainly be an added help. Perhaps the time will come when learning symbols will precede learning to read for most children. Many may even be taught to read through the use of symbols. Gwen Mann is interested in this approach. Learning to read words spelled with the abstract letters of our alphabet may seem much easier when at least some of the words are presented along with symbols that make more sense to the child.

On the other hand, some teachers are afraid that if children first learn to communicate with symbols, they will not want to tackle the harder task of learning to read words. This seems unlikely. Communication in the world of today still depends so much on the printed word. At any rate, this is another area to be explored and experimented with. Before any final decisions are made, teachers and other helpers need much more experience in using symbols with adults as well as with children.

The use of Blissymbols may also teach us something about what happens in general when people learn to communicate *visually* rather than through sounds, for there are fundamental differences in these two ways of organizing information. Some scholars think that all humans are born with an ability to differentiate objects by their shapes and outlines and to attach meaning to what they perceive in this way. This ability is seen in the drawings of young children, in which the shape of the figures is more important than the details. It may account for the children's remarkable success in understanding Blissymbols and the ease with which they learn them.

Verbal communication, on the other hand, depends on an ability to give meaning to certain sounds and organize them in understandable units. This of course became the chief means of communication among humans in very early times. But it is not available at all to the deaf and only partly to those who can hear but cannot speak. Our written language is still an expression of sounds, whereas, as we have seen, Blissymbols are purely visual.

Perhaps physically handicapped people will be the first to

communicate with symbols all around the world. Then, at last, more and more people may realize that symbols can be an important aid toward international cooperation and understanding. When that happens, the dream of Charles Bliss will be on the way to becoming a reality.

Appendix

A Sample Blissymbolics Communication Display

December, 1975; symbols updated December, 1978

zero	one	two	three
0	1	2	3
hello	question	I, me	(to) like
○→←	⌐?⌐	⊥₁	♡̂+!
goodbye	why	you	(to) want
○←→	?▷	⊥₂	♡̂?
please	how	man	(to) come
!♡	?∧	人	→̂|
thanks	who	woman	(to) give
♡⚓	?⊥	⚓̸	⚓̂
much, many	what thing	father	(to) make
×̌	?□	仌	△̂
opposite meaning	which	mother	(to) help
1	?÷	仝	∧̂|
music	where	brother	(to) think
♩♫	?̲	仌₂	⌒̂
	when	sister	(to) know
	?🕐	△̂₂	⌂̂
	how much, many	teacher	(to) wash, bathe
	?×	⊥⚓⌂	◡̂

136

four	five	six	seven	eight	nine
4	5	6	7	8	9
happy	action indicator	food	pen, pencil	friend	animal
angry	mouth	drink	paper, page	God	bird
afraid	eye	bed	book	house	flower
funny	legs and feet	toilet	table	school	water, liquid
good	hand	pain	television	hospital	sun
big	ear	clothing	news	store	weather
new	nose	outing	word	show place, theatre	day
difficult	head	motor car	light.	room	weekend
hot	name	wheelchair	toy	street	birthday

A Sample Chart for a Nonspeaking Stroke Victim

hello O →←	question ⌊?⌋
goodbye O ←→	why ?▷
please !♡	how ⌒ ?∧
thanks ♡⚓	who ?⊥
yes +!!	which ?÷
no −!!	where ?
much, many ∨ ✕	when ?🕐
(to) be ∧ Ⓓ	(to) make ∧ △
(to) have ∧ ±	conditional indicator ?

I, me	(to) come	happy	mouth	food
you	(to) go, leave	sad	eye	water, liquid
daughter	(to) like	angry	legs and feet	toilet
cousin	(to) want	lonely	hand	wheelchair
friend	(to) help	upset	ear	clothing
girl	(to) wash, bathe	sick	nose	room
boy	(to) eat	hot	head	light
nurse	(to) drink	cold	name	sun
doctor	(to) sleep	good	God	day

A Word-to-Symbol Glossary

(Symbols are shown as they appear on the symbol stamps)

a, an	(to) be able, can ∧	brother
＼	·∨	⌃2
about, of	(to) be ∧	but
＞	Φ	⊣
action indicator ∧	because	by, of
	▷?	＜
adult	bed	car, vehicle
♀	⊢⊣	⨂⨂
after, behind	before, in front of	chair
¦·	·¦	⊢
alone, only ∨	big ∨	child
Φ₁ ⓘ	I	♀
and, also	bird	city
＋	⅄	××⌂
angry ∨	body	clothing
×♡《	▢	⌗
animal	book	combine indicator ⊕
⋀⋀	▯▯	
baby	boy	(to) come ∧
⊶	⼂	→¦

140

command	earth	food	happy	it	(to) love
!	—	○	♡↑	I	–♡→
country(side)	(to) eat	foot	(to) have	(to) kiss	make-believe
	○	△	±	∞	⊕
(to) cry	excited	friend	he, him	(to) know	man
☉⤵	♡!!!	⊥♡+!	λ3	⌒	λ
daughter	eye	funny	head	(to) laugh	me, I
△	☉	♡↑○	⊥	♡↑○	⊥ₗ
day	family	girl	heart	(to) learn	milk
○	Kᴧᴧⵠ	8	♡	⚓⌒	⊘⊕
difficult	father	(to) go, leave	hello	legs and feet	money
→!	⋀	|→	○→←─	∧	8
(to) do, act	(to) feel	God	hot	light	mother
∧	♡	⚠	⟨⟩	◎	⋀
down	(to) fight	good	house	(to) like	mouth
↓	⋈	♡+!	⌂	♡+!	○
(to) drink	fire	good-bye	in, inside	little	much, many
⊘	⟩	○←─→	⊡	I	×
ear	flower	hand	intensity	lonely	no
⟩	♀	√	!	♡–⊥	–!!

nose	(to) play	(to) see	symbol display	toilet	which
not	please	she, her	(to) teach	tree	who
on	present	sick	teacher	under	who, which, that, when, where
opposite meaning	rain	similar	teenager	up	why
or	(to) read	sister	telephone	upset	woman
paper, page	room	sky	television	(to) walk, go	wow
part (of)	sad	snow	thanks	(to) want	yes
pen, pencil	(to) say, tell	star	the	water, liquid	you
person	school	sun	thing	we, us	young
pet	secret	(to) surprise	time	wheelchair	yuck

A List of Supply and Resource Centers

B.C.I. SUPPLY CENTERS

Blissymbolics materials are available only from these two sources:
Blissymbolics Communication Institute
350 Rumsey Road
Toronto, Canada, M4G IR8

EBSCO Curriculum Materials
1230 First Avenue North
Birmingham, Alabama 35203
(Call toll free: 1–800–633–8623)

(EBSCO Curriculum Materials is B.C.I.'s exclusive U.S.A. distributor.)

B.C.I. INTERNATIONAL RESOURCE CENTERS

Resource Centers, which are sublicensed by B.C.I., serve as local information centers. Here, teachers are trained in using Blissymbols, conferences are held, and Blissymbol work is carried on with nonspeaking people in demonstration projects. Centers have audio-visual materials available for use, and some of them offer consultation and assessments.

Canada

British Columbia

Rosemary Park, Director
Blissymbolics Resource Centre
Sunny Hill Hospital for
  Children
2755 East 21st Avenue
Vancouver, B.C. V5M 2W3

Ontario

Maurice Izzard, Director
Blissymbolics Resource Centre

Ontario Crippled Children's
  Centre School
350 Rumsey Road
Toronto, Ontario M4G 1R8

Quebec

Pauline Demers , Director
Blissymbolics Resource Centre
Cerebral Palsy Association of
  Quebec, Inc.
525 Boul, Hamel
Suite A 50
Quebec, P.Q. G1M 2S8

U.S.A.

Alabama

Pam Elder, Director
Blissymbolics Resource Center
DESEMO Project
University of Alabama in
　Birmingham
P.O. Box 313
University Station
Birmingham, Alabama 35294

California

Melvin Cohen, Ph.D., Director
Blissymbolics Resource Center
Dept. of Speech and Language
　Development
Communication Disorders
　Service
Medical Center
Loma Linda University
Loma Linda, California 92350

Florida

Sandra Osborn, Director
The Crippled Childrens Society
　of Orange County Florida
The Blissymbolics Resource and
　Demonstration Center
1600 Silver Star Road
Orlando, Florida 32804

Pennsylvania

E.T. McDonald, Ph.D.,
　Director
Blissymbolics Approved
　Training Center
Home of the Merciful Saviour
　for Crippled Children

4400 Baltimore Avenue
Philadelphia, Pennsylvania
　19104

Sweden

Annagreta Malmstrom-Groth,
　M.D., Director
Swedish Blissymbolics Resource
　Center
Ekhaga hab. avd.
Munkgagsg. 160
58255 Linkoping, Sweden

United Kingdom

Ena Davies, National Advisor
Blissymbolics Communication
　Resource Centre
c/o Institute of Higher
　Education
Western Avenue
Llandaff, Cardiff, Wales
United Kingdom, CF5 2YB

B.C.I. INTERNATIONAL
AFFILIATES

Canada

British Columbia

R. Alan Currie
Greater Victoria Blissymbolics
　Programme
#420–620 View Street
Victoria, B.C.

Canada *(continued)*

Newfoundland and Labrador

Sharon Foley, President
Blissymbolics Association of
  Newfoundland and Labrador
Virginia Waters School
300 Elizabeth Avenue
St. John's, Newfoundland A1B
  1T9

U.S.A.

California

Caroline Price-Clark
10854 Morrison Street, #4
North Hollywood, California
  91601

Minnesota

Roberta Kreb
Northdale Junior High School
11301 Dogwood Avenue
Coon Rapids, Minnesota 55433

Ohio

Ann Banks
Colerain Elementary School
499 East Weisheimer Road
Columbus, Ohio 43214

Wisconsin

Arthur S. Krival, Administrator
University of
  Wisconsin—Extension
Room 314 Waisman Center
1500 Highland Ave.
Madison, Wisconsin 53706

Australia

Mrs. Joan Hurren
8 Yarrow Place
O'Connor
ACT 2601
Australia

Denmark

Flemming Nielsen
Inspector
The Society and Home for
  Cripples
Geelsgaard Boarding School
Kongevejen 252
Virum, Denmark

France

André Sylvestre, Ph.D.,
Centre de Reeducation et de
  Readaptation Fonctionelles c
  Kerpape
CRF Kerpape
Lorient, France

India

Sudha Kaul
West Bengal Spastics Society
15 Belevedere Court
11/13 Alipore Road
Calcutta, India

Israel

Judy Seligman-Wine
Ramat Motza
Jerusalem, Israel

New Zealand

Bert Reeves
Matariki Physically

Handicapped Unit
Forbury School, Oxford Street
Dunedin, New Zealand

Norway

Ms. Astri Holgersen
Rektor
Trondsletten Cerebral
  Pareseinstitutt
  Skoleavdelingen
Postboks 1308
Broset Hageby
Trondheim 7001
Norway

**INFORMATION CENTERS/
COORDINATING
COMMITTEES**

Canada

Alberta

Carol Barchard
  Coordinator for Alberta
10908 126th Street
Edmonton, Alberta T5M 0P3

Nova Scotia

Laurie Waddell
Committee for the Promotion
  of Blissymbolics in Nova
  Scotia
Izaak Walton Killam Hospital
  for Children
5850 University Avenue
Halifax, Nova Scotia

U.S.A.

Michigan

Barbara Reckell
Beekman Center
MA Program
2901 Wabush Road
Lansing, Michigan 48910

Vermont

Doris J. Farenkopf
Speech Pathology
Vermont Achievement Center
88 Park Street
Rutland, Vermont 05701

Bibliography

Bliss, Charles K., *Semantography-Blissymbolics*. Sydney, Australia: Semantography Publications, 1965.

———and McNaughton, Shirley, *The Book to the Film: "Mr. Symbol Man."* Sydney, Australia: Semantography-Blissymbolics Publications, 1975.
(The two preceding books are available from: C. K. Bliss, P.O. Box 222, Coogee 2034, Sydney, Australia.)

Dreyfus, Henry, *Symbol Sourcebook: An Authoritative Guide to Graphic Symbols*. New York: McGraw Hill, 1972.

Hehner, Barbara, ed., *Blissymbols for Use*. Toronto: Blissymbolics Communication Institute, 1979. (Symbols arranged by structure and grouped according to meaning; index of English equivalents.)

McDonald, Eugene, *Teaching and Using Blissymbols*. Toronto: Blissymbolics Communication Institute, 1980.

McNaughton, Shirley, *Symbol Secrets* (juvenile). Toronto: Ontario Crippled Children's Centre, 1975.

Silverman, Franklin H., *Communication for the Speechless*. Englewood Cliffs, New Jersey: Prentice-Hall, 1979.

Silverman, Harry, McNaughton, Shirley, and Kates, Barbara, *The Handbook of Blissymbols for Instructors, Users, Parents and Administrators*. Toronto: Blissymbolics Communication Institute, 1978. (Loose-leaf, for updating.)

Vanderheiden, Gregg C., and Grilley, Kate, eds., *Non-Vocal Communication Techniques and Aids for the Severely Handicapped*. Baltimore, London, and Tokyo: University Park Press, 1976.

Index